Out of This World
Library Programs

Out of This World Library Programs

Using Speculative Fiction to Promote Reading and Launch Learning

Joel A. Nichols

Foreword by Denise E. Agosto

LIBRARIES UNLIMITED™
An Imprint of ABC-CLIO, LLC
Santa Barbara, California • Denver, Colorado

Out of This World Library Programs: Using Speculative Fiction to Promote Reading and Launch Learning
Library of Congress Cataloging in Publication Control Number: 2016048094

ISBN: 978–1–4408–5286–2
EISBN: 978–1–4408–5287–9

21 20 19 18 17   1 2 3 4 5

This book is also available as an eBook.

Libraries Unlimited
An Imprint of ABC-CLIO, LLC

ABC-CLIO, LLC
130 Cremona Drive, P.O. Box 1911
Santa Barbara, California 93116-1911
www.abc-clio.com

This book is printed on acid-free paper ∞

Manufactured in the United States of America

Contents

Foreword

"Speculative fiction"—just the phrase itself sets the mind awhirl with possibility. The term has generated decades of controversy. Does speculative fiction encapsulate all of both science fiction and fantasy, or just parts? Does it include anything else? And what makes science fiction science fiction? What makes fantasy fantasy? What is the difference between fantasy and science fiction? Literature fans and literature critics alike have argued over these questions for decades, but in truth, the name and breadth of the genre matters much less than its effect on readers.

And that effect is to promote dreaming and wonder. Speculative fiction makes us *think*—really think—about new ideas and new possibilities. Its power to provoke creative and critical thinking is equally strong for children, adolescents, and adults. In this exciting new book, Joel Nichols offers 51 innovative library programs that children's and teen librarians can use to harness the power of speculative fiction to make youth think. The content of this volume goes beyond merely recommending hot new titles for children and teens to clearly laying out a range of interactive programs that can bring speculative fiction to life for young thinkers and dreamers. Speculative fiction is a natural partner for both active and passive library programming, and Joel Nichols gives us a host of ideas for basing library programs around books that children and teens are sure to love reading, interacting with, and thinking about in creative new ways.

But why should youth librarians work hard to offer thoughtful, well-designed library programs in the first place? The answer to this question lies in the history of programming in U.S. public libraries. Both adult and youth programming have been a mainstay of U.S. (and British) public library services for about the last century. Youth programming has an especially active and vibrant history, with story times and other book- and storytelling-based programs comprising the bulk of children's and teens' programs from the earliest days of public library programming right up to today. Across the nation there has been a drastic increase in library programming offerings and attendance over the past decade or so. In fiscal year 2013, the most recent year for which statistics are currently available, there were 67.4 million attendees at children's library programs in the United States, which represented a 10-year increase of 29.7 percent in children's program attendance (IMLS 2016).

Although dedicated teen services are somewhat newer than dedicated children's services, many public libraries also offer programming for tweens and teens. In fact, a 2012 survey of 1,832 public libraries in the United States and Canada found that 82 percent offered dedicated services for teens, and among those libraries, 90 percent had offered programs geared toward teens during the previous year (Agosto 2013a). In terms of numbers, there were 6.1 million attendees at teen programs, representing a two-year increase of 15.2 percent (IMLS 2016) and auguring a continued upward trend in teen programming offerings and attendance.

This upward trend might seem surprising in light of frequent popular media portrayals of preteens and teens as more interested in participating in online worlds than in the everyday physical world. Indeed, in today's highly networked world, where technology is changing the face of daily communication, why *do* story times and other book-based programs remain so popular in public libraries? The answer is simple: library programming (when thoughtfully designed and carefully delivered) can lead to a host of benefits to participants, benefits that extend beyond the library context into nearly every aspect of youths' lives.

In their popular teen library services guide *Connecting Young Adults and Libraries: A How-to-Do-It Manual for Librarians*, Patrick Jones, Michele Gorman, and Tricia Suellentrop (2009) list six benefits of library programming for teens (and for the library as well). They write that programming will:

- Increase use of the collection and other core services;
- Inform, entertain, and enrich teens;
- Attract new users or convince current users to use the library differently;
- Promote the library in a positive light in the community;
- Increase youth involvement opportunities; and
- Support healthy youth development (p. 223).

This list of programming benefits emphasizes entertainment and collection use as primary reasons to offer library programs for youth. However, literacy development, digital skills building, oral and written communication skills building, and social skills development are additional benefits that are all equally important outcomes. In this book, author Joel Nichols recognizes this broader range of positive outcomes for youth and does an excellent job of showing which of these outcomes can be expected from each of the speculative fiction-based programs he outlines.

As indicated in the above list of benefits by Jones, Gorman, and Suellentrop, youth library programs are not just beneficial for youth development but for library promotion as well. An influential IMLS report (2014) that examined public library programming across the United States linked an increase in library programming to an increase in both physical visits to libraries and to the circulation of books and other library materials.

All this is to say that library programs help to educate, inform, and entertain library users while giving them extra reasons and reminders to visit and use their libraries.

I should also point out that *Out of This World Library Programs: Using Speculative Fiction to Promote Reading and Launch Learning* comes at a period of fundamental change in U.S. public library services for children and teens. In line with a growing focus on libraries as active centers of community engagement and interaction, youth librarians across the country are devoting increasing time, effort, and resources to developing and delivering a broader range of library programs than ever before. Most of these forward-thinking youth librarians have moved away from thinking about collections as the core focus of library services to thinking about creating positive impacts on youths' lives as the ultimate goal of library programs and services. Each of the program descriptions in this book includes expected learning outcomes—specific social, emotional, and cognitive benefits to young participants—thereby enabling program developers to choose programs not just according to which ones look to be the most fun or the most exciting, but according to which ones can meet predetermined developmental outcome goals.

This book also comes at a time when youth librarians across the United States are moving their services ever deeper into the digital world, focusing more on collecting and promoting digital resources and on using networked tools and platforms to engage and interact with young library users. Despite this growing emphasis on the digital world, U.S. public librarians continue to stress the value of the physical library as a place for children and teens (and adults, of course!) to frequent for individual and collaborative use, and many librarians are thinking about the importance of the library as place even more strongly than in the past (Agosto 2016). The speculative fiction-based programs presented here take advantage of the lasting power of the physical library as an ideal place for promoting strong social, intellectual, and emotional benefits for youth, many of whom lack access to other noncommercial, youth-friendly gathering spaces in their communities.

There is yet an additional reason to offer youth library programming with speculative fiction, a reason that youth librarians should find especially compelling: these programs can help today's children and teens to understand the ongoing relevance of public libraries in the modern information world, a world filled with digital information and digital information systems. My recent research with high school students across the country has shown that, tragically, many of today's teens share "a widely held perception that 'libraries' represent an outdated past, whereas 'technology' represents teens' everyday reality. Few [see] libraries as relevant to their daily lives, yet most [see] social media as relevant" (Agosto, Magee, Dickard, and Forte 2016).

Sadly, this means that many youth growing up in today's technology-focused information environments tend to view libraries as dusty book warehouses, out of touch with their technology-filled lives. We in the library field know that libraries and technology are complementary, not competing, entities, but that message just isn't getting through to most youth. As a field, youth librarians need to work hard to fight this misperception of libraries as mere paper book warehouses. If we as a profession hope to continue to make strong positive impacts on youths' lives, we must help larger numbers of youth to develop deeper awareness, interest, and enthusiasm in their libraries. Speculative fiction-based programming offers us a powerful hook for doing just that.

The future of youth library services is now in our hands. I invite you to read this book and to take advantage of the many important programs and lessons it provides about how to excite today's youth about today's libraries while also providing youth with important opportunities for improved social, emotional, and cognitive development. You, your library, and the youth in your community have much to benefit from your doing so.

Denise E. Agosto, Ph.D.
Professor and Director, Master's of Library & Information Science
Program College of Computing & Informatics
Drexel University, Philadelphia, PA

NOTE

Although much of the writing about library services for adolescent populations uses the term "young adults" to refer to youth ages 12–18, I prefer the terms "teens" or "teenagers." Teens themselves commonly use these terms for self-reference, whereas "young adult" is a term used almost exclusively by librarians and publishers. For an extended discussion of these various terms and their use in library literature and practice, see Denise E. Agosto, "Envisaging Young Adult Librarianship from a Teen-Centered Perspective" (pp. 33–52), in *Transforming Young Adult Services* (Chicago: Neal-Schuman, 2013).

REFERENCES

Agosto, Denise E. 2013a. "The Big Picture of YA Services: Analyzing the Results of the 2012 PLA PLDS Survey." *Young Adult Library Services* 11(3): 13–18.

Agosto, Denise E. 2013b. "Envisaging Young Adult Librarianship from a Teen-Centered Perspective" (pp. 33–52), in *Transforming Young Adult Services*. Chicago: Neal-Schuman.

Agosto, Denise E. 2016. "Hey! The Library Is Kind of Awesome!" Current Trends in U.S. Public Library Services for Teens. Address at the 10th International Symposium on Library Services for Children and Young Adults, in Seoul, South Korea, June 28, 2016.

Agosto, Denise E., Rachel M. Magee, Michael Dickard, and Andrea Forte. 2016. "Teens, Technology, and Libraries: An Uncertain Relationship." *Library Quarterly* 86(3): 248–269.

IMLS. 2014. *Public Libraries in the United States Survey.* http://www.imls.gov/research/public_libraries_in_the_us_fy_2012_report.aspx.

IMLS. 2016. *Public Libraries in the United States Survey.* https://www.imls.gov/sites/default/files/publications/documents/plsfy2013.pdf.

Jones, Patrick, Michele Gorman, and Tricia Suellentrop. 2009. *Connecting Young Adults and Libraries: A How-to-Do-It Manual for Librarians.* New York: Neal-Schuman Publishers.

Part One

BACKGROUND

Introduction

Source: Vintageprintable1-Art - Stamp Art - Russia - Sputnik - USSR 1967 - Science Fiction/Creative Commons license. https://www.flickr.com/photos/vintageprint abledotcom/4967208776.

This book is intended to serve as a programming and genre guide for librarians working with teens and tweens. The book features more than 50 ready-made program plans librarians can use with young people in a public or school library setting that rely on and stimulate interest in speculative literature and geek culture.

Each program plan is structured around specific books and stories, and also offers suggestions for further reading and other media that practitioners can use to adapt these plans. This book features a wide range of texts and other media in science fiction literature, fantasy literature, and their many speculative and fantastical subgenres, and the terms science fiction, fantasy, sci-fi, SF, and SFF are used somewhat interchangeably here.

The genre guide aims to be descriptive and selective rather than exhaustive: that is, the short stories, books, and DVDs constitute a diverse and wide range of speculative fiction, but the book does not try to present every single title of interest in the way a comprehensive readers' advisory genre guide might. Instead, this book gives librarians who may or may not be fans of these genres the most interesting, most compelling, and in many cases most accessible titles across this vast and varied area of imaginative literature and media. There is a special emphasis on media and books created by women and people of color, both because they are excellent works and because those are two groups especially underrepresented in speculative fiction and fantasy literatures and media.

Each program plan features texts and activities, and touches many key literacies. The primary kinds of skills practiced again and again in these are programs are:

- **Research and information literacy instruction:** Many of the programs require participants to find additional examples, particular video clips, identify official Twitter accounts, use message boards and wikis, and discern sources. Feel free to add and adapt based on your style of information literacy instruction.
- **Crafts and projects:** There are tangible products in many programs, many of which I encourage you to leave on display in the library. The art projects and many drawings and sketches can be adapted for any medium available—that is, from clay tablets to iPads! Additional resources, such as e-textiles and working with LEDs, can be added as you see appropriate. And they all work with pencils and scrap paper, too.
- **Writing exercises:** Practicing writing in a non-school environment can be a turnoff to some teens, so be sure to stress that all the writing produced in these programs is for fun, and let participants share or hold back as they see fit. In these programs, librarians and teachers can find ways to help participants practice letters, reviews, blogs, tweets, short stories, epics, sonnets, and more. These are not meant to replicate a fiction workshop, but rather demonstrate the key skills and, most importantly, let the teens iterate.
- **Digital projects:** Some of the programs require tablets or laptops, for things like stop-motion animation, graphic design, photos, or podcasts. Many of them can be carried out in modified form with reduced or even no technology, and I encourage you to reduce or enhance of the levels of sophistication based on the technology available.
- **STEM:** In the preschool programming section, you have a great opportunity to lay a groundwork for SFF programs by using

STEM/STEAM content. In addition, there are many thematic connections to real-life science—for example, cloning, robotics, space exploration, and others.

HOW TO USE THE PROGRAM PLANS

Each program plan has the following components:

Goals: The overarching précis that states the scope and the point of the program.

Primary Books and Media: These suggestions are based on books I am familiar with and have successfully shared with others. In many cases, you may not have the time to share an entire book with your group of participants. I have attempted to distill the most crucial reasons behind my choice and suggest which selections to share. As always, substitute in books you know and love as appropriate.

Additional Books and Media: In many cases, I have chosen popular and widely seen films and TV shows that many participants will be familiar with, and which will be easy to locate on DVD or in clip form online. In this section, you'll also find alternatives based on the age of the participant, as well as additional titles in case the primary suggestions are not available in your library. Children's librarians are encouraged to select additional picture books and use themes.

Learning Objectives: Always written with the form "Participants will," this point captures the specific learning goals for each program and what skills the program participants will practice. If there are tangible products (a redesigned book cover, a Twitter feed, etc.), they are also listed here.

Duration: In hours, this describes how long the program should take. These are estimates that could vary widely in your context, depending on number of participants, for example, or whether you add additional technology or texts. Many workshops work better in shorter meetings over several days. Use your judgment about structuring these. In the long days of summer reading, you might want a program that lasts longer or takes place over more days than in the afterschool program block.

Materials Needed: Assume that participants always need scrap paper and pencils, and whatever other drawing supplies are appropriate. In addition, this section lists other items or resources you should prepare and have on hand in advance of the program. Food always helps, too, although specific food suggestions are not provided, except for the program called "*Gagh*, Soylent Green, and ChickieNobs." However, a bag of popcorn and some seltzer water can never hurt.

Instructions: This section describes what you, as program facilitator, should do. It is written for you and to you, and it tries to lay out, step-by-step, what these program plans are meant to do, and how you can conduct these programs. Use these instructions as guideposts.

A NOTE ON PROGRAMMING WITH TEENS AND TWEENS

Teens and tweens probably already use your library. Attracting them to programs can be an opportunity for you to reach current users in a deeper way, and also leverage them to attract their friends and classmates to a new kind of program at the library. The key to programming with teens and tweens is to take them seriously, and to offer them choice in what you do, and with which books or movies. These program plans provide frameworks, instructions, and specific examples you can use to present these to young adult audiences in the library. But I think the magic in being a programming librarian means being able to combine and recombine your skills, interests, and resources in different ways to meet the needs of your community. There are two approaches I recommend. The first is to preselect three or four program plans, present them with a one- or two-sentence description, and let your teens choose. The second is to select one program, but enroll your audience in selecting the books, stories, movies, or TV shows you will use as primary texts.

The following books did not fit neatly into the program plans in this book, but I want to highlight them as additional examples of science fiction and fantasy for teens and young adults:

Alanna: The First Adventure (Song of the Lioness, #1) by Tamora Pierce.
Baltimore Vol. 3: A Passing Stranger and Other Stories by Mike Mignola and
    Christopher Golden.
Beastkeeper by Cat Hellisen.
Breath of Bones: A Tale of the Golem by Steve Niles. Illus. by Dave Wachter.
The Darkest Part of the Forest by Holly Black.
The Freedom Maze by Delia Sherman.
The Giver by Lois Lowry.
The Golden Compass by Philip Pullman.
Graceling by Kristin Cashore.
Howl's Moving Castle (Howl's Moving Castle, #1) by Diana Wynne Jones.
The Madman's Daughter by Megan Shepherd.
Parasite by Mira Grant.
Rook by Sharon Cameron.
Scarlet by Marissa Meyer.

The Shadow Hero by Gene Luen Yang.
Tender Morsels by Margo Lanagan.
Through The Woods by Emily Carroll.
Trillium by Jeff Lemire.

Most importantly, find out from your young patrons what they are interested in, obsessed with, provoked by, and currently watching, reading, and playing. Let them guide your collection development, if you do not already, by tasking them with reading book reviews or selecting from online lists and giving you—and their fellow library users—feedback on what they want.

Part Two

TEENS AND TWEENS

Book Covers: Redesigning Bias

An intoxicating unreliable narrator spins a sad, terrifying tale that crosses from the realism of a teen in trouble to the fantastical—or does it? The tension of whether or not this character is (minor spoiler alert) a werewolf, and what that has to do with her present lies, drives this book forward. In real life, it is also a problematic portrayal of a young woman of color by a white author (who since regrets it—see "On White Fragility" by Larbalestier, http://readingwhilewhite.blogspot.com/2016/08/on-white-fragility-by-guest-blogger.html). In addition, the publisher tried to publish it with a cover image that did not represent the character.

Goals: Teens learn about book marketing and design, and how bias can occur in design, and explore ways to overcome bias in design.

Primary Books and Media: *Liar* by Justine Larbalestier. This teen novel features an unforgettable unreliable narrator who is at the very least a deeply troubled young woman trying to negotiate her life, and at the most perhaps a werewolf. Or not. She is definitely supposed to be a young woman of color, but the publisher (infamously) tried to put as the cover image a young woman who was very fair and conformed to white beauty standards.

Additional Books and Media: *If You Come Softly* by Jacqueline Woodson; *I Am the Cheese* by Robert Cormier; *Monster* by Walter Dean Myers; *The Hunger Games* by Suzanne Collins; *Pretty Little Liars* by Sara Shepard; *The Kane Chronicles* (any of them) by Rick Riordan; *White Cat* by Holly Black; *A Wizard of Earthsea* by Ursula K. Le Guin.

Learning Objectives: Participants will

- Learn about design elements of a book, and how cover design is part of a process; gain experience putting design principles into practice
- Engage in books they have an interest in

Duration: 3 hours, approximately

Materials Needed:

- Images of *Liar* original cover image and redesigned one (Google image search)
- Find an article that addresses this practice to guide and spark discussion. Google search "whitewashing book covers" or use these:
  - http://www.slj.com/2014/05/diversity/bank-street-school-librarian -shares-her-year-long-lesson-in-diversity-in-childrens-books
  - http://www.yalsa.ala.org/thehub/2012/12/10/it-matters-if -youre-black-or-white-the-racism-of-ya-book-covers/
  - http://www.theguardian.com/books/2015/nov/18/rick-riordan -publisher-dropping-cover-whitewashing-black-hero-kane -chronicles
- Copies of the book *Liar* and/or other teen novels by some of the writers listed above (one per participant, although students could work in pairs, or two individuals could work on the same book cover)
- Computers or tablets: either reserve a couple of library computers, especially if the students are working in pairs, or encourage them to bring their own tablets if available
- Photo editor software (such as Photoshop) or Web tools (e.g., Paint, GIMP, or even Microsoft Publisher or PowerPoint) to edit photos and text

Let students know that this is for practice, and that they won't be publishing any images, so they are free to use and remix copyrighted materials they find in Google image search. If you or they do intend to publish or use these materials, they should be sure to be searching for Creative Commons images (see note on Creative Commons on p. 57) or other materials they have permissions to modify.

Or you can use:

- Images from teen magazines such as *Tiger Beat, Kiki, Seventeen,* or *Teen Vogue,* or from book catalogues that have many cover images, or even images printed from the Internet so participants have a wide variety of materials and images to collage from
- Scissors, glue sticks, and paper

Instructions:

- Explain the original cover and design controversy.
- Ask participants, What do you think? How does this cover represent you and your communities?

- Direct each participant to find a book cover that could use a more inclusive design.
- Redesign: use paper/paste or any digital solution. Depending on the software or supplies available in your library, lead the participants through a redesign. Tell them to take 1 hour to complete their project.
- When finished, have participants vote for best redesign: which new book cover best represents the characters and the way the author wanted them to look? How does it compare to the original?

Frankentoys: Mashed-Up Monsters That Teach Descriptive Vocabulary

Action figures are a mainstay of geek culture, with figurines and other toys from franchises from *Firefly* to the Justice League. This program is an opportunity to deconstruct and reconstruct them into new and weird creations, with participants trying out their best character designs.

Goals: Create custom action figures that represent aliens or monsters from fiction, and increase vocabulary skills.

Primary Books and Media: *Perdido Street Station* by China Miéville; *Dawn* by Octavia Butler.

Miéville's *Perdido Street Station* takes place in a world called Bas-Lag, which is also the home to two of his other novels, *Iron Council* and *The Scar*. Bas-Lag is a secondary world where humans coexist with other sentient creatures: the Khepri, who have cockroach heads and women's bodies, the Cactacae, who live in a Victorian greenhouse, the frog-like Vodyanoi, and so on. In addition to these strange species and types, the book describes a form of punishment where someone's body is "remade" by grafting it to a machine in some horrendous way. Legs might be replaced by steam-powered wheels, for example.

Octavia Butler's *Dawn* is the first of a three-book series about mysterious, ancient aliens finding Earth after humans have nearly destroyed themselves with atomic war. These aliens, the Oankali, are master manipulators of their environments and of genetics. They come in three sex/gender types and are covered in tentacles that act as sensory organs but also carry a deadly sting. One of their gender types, the ooloi, has a special arm with hands and fingers shaped like a flower or starfish. In addition to these strange types, there are living houses that respond to chemical signals, and other plants and animals that have been modified to be like giant motorized walkways and living spaceships, and in the later books, Oankali-human hybrids. The first chapter of *Dawn*—when Lilith first sees an Oankali—has rich description of them.

Additional Books and Media: *A Miracle of Rare Design* by Mike Resnick; *The Madman's Daughter* by Megan Shepherd.

Learning Objectives: Participants will

- Practice reading descriptions of imaginary and unusual beings
- Learn a new DIY art skill by translating an unfamiliar description into a toy sculpture

Duration: 3 hours, approximately

Materials Needed:

- Large selection of action figures, dolls, Barbies, toy cars, and other assorted toys. These materials are easier to work with when they are already broken or missing pieces, so feel free to collect assorted pieces from thrift stores or solicit donations for broken toys/pieces. Take care to sort through them for anything sharp, electronic, or dangerous. Depending on the age of participants, you may want to disassemble the action figures in advance with very sharp scissors or a knife.
- Glue. Superglue works best, although a hot glue gun is sufficient.
- Scotch tape
- Scrap paper and crayons

Instructions:

- Read selections from the texts described above, picking out the paragraphs that best describe the physicality of the aliens or beings.
- Be ready to define words, and pick out unusual descriptors they may find unfamiliar to highlight: gelatinous, for example, or chitinous, bulbous, striated, and so forth.
- Brainstorm, as a group, what other aliens, monsters, or creatures they have seen or read about in other movies, TV shows, or books. Challenge each participant to add a descriptive word or phrase to the creature they have named.
- Read two or three of the same selections from the books above, and ask the participants to do a one-minute sketch of what you described.
- Share the sketches, reinforcing the descriptors you have defined or highlighted, and also the ones from the brainstorm.

- Put the action figures and toy pieces in a pile everyone has access to. Allow everyone to take one piece at a time, and rotate around the table until everyone has five pieces.
- Ask participants to build their own Frankentoy. Depending on the materials available, they can try to make one of China Miéville's or Octavia Butler's creations, or make up their own.
- They should begin laying out and fitting their pieces together. After 5 minutes or so, let them take more pieces from the pile as necessary. They can "storyboard" their figures with Scotch tape while they make final adjustments.
- This works best if an adult can help with gluing.
- When everyone has finished or when the time is up, take pictures of the toys if you can, and ask each participant to write the name of the creature and up to three descriptors as a label. You can display these Frankentoys (or pictures of them) in the library for a few days, then let their makers take them home.

So Real They're on Twitter!: Superhero Micro-Blogging and More

Twitter is alive with science fiction and fantasy writers, and is a place where fans and critics alike can have direct interaction with the authors they read, study, idolize, or even detest. There is a huge thrill when a writer acknowledges you on Twitter by liking a tweet or retweeting something you have written. This program is also a good opportunity to talk about privacy and online harassment, as SFF writers—especially women and people of color—have been targeted on Twitter with threats.

Goals: Create a Twitter feed, blog, or faux Facebook page as a superhero or other well-known character.

Primary Books and Media: Any superhero graphic novel; video clips from superhero movies or TV shows; *Feed* by M. T. Anderson, a haunting YA novel from 2002 that presciently dramatizes what it would be like if teenagers had social media implanted in their brains and were always online.

Additional Books and Media: *Uglies* by Scott Westerfeld; *Will Grayson, Will Grayson* by John Green and David Levithan; *Smallville* episode "Upgrade," season 9, episode 17 (http://smallville.wikia.com/wiki/Upgrade).

Learning Objectives: Participants will

- Learn how to set up a social media profile and create themed content
- Learn how to write within the confines of a 140-character limit
- Reflect on privacy and identity on social media

Duration: 1 hour, approximately

Materials Needed:

- Computers or tablets, if registering real accounts. If students are too young, or if there is not computer time available, use paper and pen.
- Live access to Twitter or screenshots/printouts of the Twitter feeds from fictional or historical people. Some good ones to start with: a fake Harry Potter (@ArryPottah), Bender the robot from the cartoon *Futurama* (@Bender), William Shakespeare (@Shakespeare), and the official fake Katniss Everdeen (@Katniss). Be sure to double-check these sample tweets and feeds for age-appropriate content.

Instructions:

- Explain micro-blogging and Twitter, and discuss the examples.
- Explain that RT means retweet, or reblog the content; DM means a private, direct message; tagging someone else engages them: it is a way to get them to notice what you are posting, or to indicate that they were with you, and so forth. Remind them that you can tweet GIFs, pictures, links, and so on.
- Ask participants to share their favorite tweets from the samples.
- Tell them that they are going to pick a character and write some tweets to get their character's feed started. When everyone has chosen a character (either one they know well from previous media, or a superhero in one of the graphic novels available in the program), either direct them to a computer and to twitter.com to sign up and chose a handle or have them write it out on paper.
- Have participants choose an image to use as their avatar.
- Make a list of the Twitter handles they have chosen, and share it where everyone can see.
- Direct them to write up to 10 tweets. Use these questions and prompts to get them writing:
  - What did your character's morning look like? What time did the character wake up? Did the character drink coffee or tea? What was the weather like? Did the character have to go anywhere?
  - What was your character's last meal at a restaurant? Describe it. Find or draw a picture of it.
  - Think of something that has been in the news in the last couple weeks. What would your character say about it? What kind of Internet link would the character share about it?
  - Who are the other people or beings the hero might talk to on a given day? Who is your character's best friend? What about a nemesis or another villain: would such an antagonist have anything to say to the hero?

- Where has the character been recently, for work or on vacation? Check the character into airports he or she might have been passing through (unless the hero is flying there with superpowers!)
  - It is Friday night and the hero doesn't have anyone to save. What does the character do to have fun and relax?
- If using actual Twitter accounts, encourage participants to post several of their tweets, and encourage them to tag and RT the fictional accounts of fellow participants so they can engage in a robust Twitter conversation.
- In conclusion, bring the participants back together to discuss what it was like to create a persona on social media. Ask them if there is anything private they know their character would never share? How do they think about their own privacy on Instagram or Twitter?
- This is a good time to demonstrate the privacy settings on Twitter, where appropriate.

Authors Are People Too: Fan Letters and Sci-Fi Fandom

Having a favorite or famous author notice you on Twitter is one tiny corner of fandom, a tradition that developed out of science fiction conventions, fan newsletters, and communities of fans coalescing around a franchise such as Star Wars or Star Trek. Before Twitter, fans wrote letters and sometimes the writers even wrote back. If participants are interested, encourage them to find examples of responses from golden age or new wave science fiction writers.

Goals: Learn about SF fandom and fan letters and practice writing by drafting and/or sending a fan letter.

Primary Books and Media: *Letters to Tiptree*, edited by Alisa Krasnostein and Alexandra Pierce, an anthology of "fan" letters from SF authors to Alice Sheldon's James Tiptree persona. (See the "All about Tiptree: Inventing a Literary Alter Ego" chapter for more information about Tiptree.) Also, *Afterworlds* by Scott Westerfeld.

Additional Books and Media: Blog post with images of fan letters from early SF magazines (https://betweenthecoversblog.wordpress.com/2012/02/10/wonder-stories-and-the-superfan/); Tor.com sample from *Letters to Tiptree* (http://www.tor.com/2015/08/12/excerpts-letters-to-tiptree-brit-mandelo/).

Learning Objectives: Participants will

- Improve comprehension skills by reading sample fan letters
- Identify an SF author they would like to contact
- Learn how to draft and send a letter or email to an author

Duration: 3 hours, approximately

Materials Needed:

- Computers/tablets, paper/pencils, whiteboard, or some other way to take notes and share them with participants

Instructions:

- Explain that fandom and fan letters—especially in letters to early science fiction magazines—were a form of social networking and literary critique that connected readers with each other, and also with the authors. The communities and newsletters and other publications that grew out of this culture of fan letters also influenced the development of fan fiction. In fan fiction, amateur writers use the characters and worlds created by others to further and continue the story.
- Talk about *Letters to Tiptree*, emphasizing that this book is a collection of current SFF writers who are writing to a hero and idol of theirs who is long dead. So they are of course using the form of a letter to talk to and be in conversation with other fans.
- Read a sample from the Tiptree book. SF writer and critic Brit Mandelo's letter is reprinted at the Tor.com blog for reference (http://www.tor.com/2015/08/12/excerpts-letters-to-tiptree-brit-mandelo/).
- Ask participants about the last good SFF books they read, and what their favorites are. What authors have they returned to again and again? What authors did they find impossible to understand or get into? Why?
- Direct participants to take 7 minutes to browse the library collection and find SFF books they have enjoyed, are interested in, have questions about, would like to recommend, and so forth. It is not necessary for the participants to have actually read the author, although they will have a richer experience if they do. Encourage them to start reading the first chapter, and give these participants time to do so.
- Bring the group back together, and ask them to name their author and pose one question they have about the book, the character, and so on. Record these on a whiteboard or butcher paper on the wall.
- Conduct another round, prompting the group to describe one thing they really like or enjoy or are interested in about these authors or in these books. Record these on the whiteboard.
- Direct participants to write a dear author letter, refining their questions and describing to the author what they like about the book.
- Remind them that they can add and write more: additional questions of the author, clarifying any ambiguities in the book or story, critiques, and so on.

- Let the group draft these letters for 15 or 20 minutes, then bring them back together to read them (or portions of them, time-depending) in the group.
- If you intend to actually attempt to contact authors, demonstrate how to find an author's website and official contact information, if available. Be prepared for these to be Web forms, generic emails, comment boxes, and so forth. Students might also look for them on Twitter.
- If actually sending these letters, take the time to write and polish one or two more drafts. Encourage students to read their whole letter aloud to another participant to check for typos and errors.
- Participants should feel free to use dead authors, as in the sample to Tiptree. But living authors might actually write (or tweet) back!

Claymation Adaptation

Designed in collaboration with Scott Oskin, school library media specialist, Boston Public Schools, when we worked together at Charles Durham Neighborhood Library, Free Library of Philadelphia.

Animating with clay gets participants using their hands as well as their heads, as they both craft their characters and scenes with modeling clay and plan out the shots of their movie on a storyboard. This animation is labor intensive and detail-oriented, and this program chunks it into workshops that both build on each other and can accommodate participants stopping in for the first time. These techniques can be adapted to serve many subjects and themes in addition to science fiction and fantasy.

Goals: To recreate an action scene from a movie or book.

Primary Books and Media: *The Hunger Games* by Suzanne Collins (consider showing clips of the movie); *Jurassic Park* by Michael Crichton and clips from the movie *Jurassic Park* or one of its sequels. This program relies on finding an action sequence that is interesting and dynamic, but not too complicated to replicate in stop-motion with clay. From *Harry Potter*, any Quidditch-playing or broom-flying sequence would work. From *Jurassic Park*, any sequence with dinosaurs should do.

Additional Books and Media: For younger participants, *Adventure Time* (cartoon series) and *Adventure Time with Fionna & Cake* by Natasha Allegri. Also Pokémon (any video or book); *Six of Crows* by Leigh Bardugo.

Learning Objectives: Participants will

- Learn to storyboard
- Practice and learn stop-motion video techniques

Duration: 2-hour workshops over several days/weeks; 10–12 hours total

Materials Needed:

- Selections from books above to read aloud/together with group
- Video clips from the movies/series above
- Tablet or phone with a stop-motion video app, such as iMotion HD
- Modeling clay; clay tools (optional; even disposal chopsticks could do)
- Storyboard template (Google image search "storyboard template" for best results)

Note: This works best in teams/small groups. When filming begins, each team needs access to a tablet or other camera.

Instructions: In a series of 2-hour after-school workshops, students will progress through a series of activities that will teach them the process of making a Claymation film.

"Story and Storyboarding"

- Begin by reading the action sequence you have chosen from one of the books above. With very young participants, this should be limited to a very simple sequence, such as one character running, jumping, or spinning, a vehicle taking off or landing, and so forth.
- Introduce the concept of storyboarding, where they will use a template to break the sequence into smaller parts. *Note:* It may be helpful to model a storyboard together, and to reinforce it by watching a clip of the same or a similar sequence. Allow participants to draw and write through the storyboard. Tell them that they will eventually be making this come alive frame by frame, so the more they can break the sequence into smaller and smaller moves, the more fluid the animation.
- Distribute clay, and let them begin shaping characters to practice.

"Clay Play"

- Walk participants through creating a series of simple shapes: a ball, a worm or snake shape, a cube, the clay totally flattened against the table, and so forth.
- If tools are available, let them practice scoring component clay pieces and joining them, as well as making fine moves.
- By the end of this session, they should start creating their characters. Sometimes, this works best in teams.

"Morph!"

- The goal of this session is to teach the principal of Claymation/stop-motion. Demonstrate the app, and consider making a sample movie. An excellent demonstration exercise is turning a ball of clay into a

Source: https://pixabay.com/en/carnotauro-dinosaur-toy-724101/.

"puddle" of clay flattened against the table. It is a simple animation to prepare in advance, and a good one for them to practice.

"Move!"

- Have participants block out their sequences with their clay figures, and start to film their action scenes. Leave plenty of time for painstaking, frame-by-frame detail.
- Circulate to help participants think through any challenges that arise. If working with very young children, feel free to actively help with the camera/app.
- At the end, be sure to export finished animations from the app into a format for saving/sharing.

"Festival"

- Present all the finished sequences for a library audience. Each team should introduce their film and sequence, talk about its inspiration from the books above, and answer any audience questions.

Steampunk Jewelry

Steampunk is both a world-building technique and, in a somewhat watered-down pop-culture way, a personal style of dress that encompasses everything from Victorian to the Wild West, with plenty of divergence. This program introduces participants to some of the main ingredients and characteristics of steampunk as an SFF setting and universe, and allows them to make a fun piece of costume jewelry.

Goals: To expose participants to the genre of steampunk and its aesthetic trappings and create a jewelry craft inspired by the genre.

Primary Books and Media: *The Golden Compass* by Philip Pullman; *Dreadnought* by Cherie Priest; *Leviathan* by Scott Westerfeld; *Steampunk* by Jeff and Ann VanderMeer; *Sherlock Holmes* (2009 film); *Warehouse 13* (TV series).

Additional Books and Media: For very young participants, *The Invention of Hugo Cabret* by Brian Selznick; *The Giant Seed* by Arthur Geisert.

Steampunk is, at this point, a sci-fi subgenre that is concerned with its gaslight and clockwork aesthetic more than its interesting world-building implications about how our society would be different if we had continued developing technology with nineteenth-century power sources. The works of Cherie Priest are faithful to this world building and approach the looks of the era with a playful tone. Scott Westerfeld's *Leviathan* and its two sequels push steampunk aesthetics even further, dividing the European powers into two groups based on whether they create coal and steam-powered machines (the Clankers) or bioengineer organisms (the Darwinists) as their preferred technologies. Find descriptions of clothes and people in these texts to inspire this project.

Learning Objectives: Participants will

- Learn about steampunk
- Produce a jewelry craft

Duration: 3 hours, approximately

Materials Needed:

- Hot glue gun and glue
- Jewelry-making supplies: buy starter supplies such as large key rings, beading string or wire, and pin-backs from a craft store or website
- Have copies of some of Westerfeld's books, such as *Leviathan*, on hand as well

This craft works best when you have a variety of unusual and strange things to choose from, so consider:

- Having a "broken jewelry" drive box at the library, where people can donate single earrings and broken bracelets
- Buying or collecting screws, nuts, bolts, and other small hardware supplies
- Scavenging a thrift store for broken jewelry, clocks, toys, or other things like small springs, gears, or screws you can disassemble and use

Instructions:

- Introduce steampunk. Here is a website (http://www.ministryof peculiaroccurrences.com/what-is-steampunk/) and a Pinterest link (https://www.pinterest.com/explore/steampunk/) you may want to show, if applicable, or review beforehand, for definitions and examples.
- Read selections from the texts or show film clips. Ask participants to share other examples from stories, TV shows, video games, graphic novels, and so on that they are familiar with. If applicable, send them into the collection to find examples (or have any examples of steampunk graphic novels, books, or media from your collection on display).
- Show the illustrations from Westerfeld's books.
- Have participants design a piece of jewelry that a steampunk character would wear. Ask them to consider their character: How old is the character? What is the character's job? Does this piece of jewelry have special meaning? Is it a special technology itself?
- They should start by sketching their idea. Then, distribute the supplies and ask them to make a "3D sketch" or prototype where they put together a concept without gluing it.
- When they are happy with their "3D sketch," they can glue it together. Depending on the age of the participants, you might do this yourself or ask another adult to help.
- Take photographs of all the steampunk pieces for display, sharing on social media, and so forth.

Strange Maps

There is nothing quite like a book that starts with a series of maps and figures describing the strange, alien, or historical geographies in which the story will take place. With their mysterious and inventive place names that hint at the plot intrigue and world building to come, strange maps help transport the reader into a new universe before the story even begins. This project can be scaled up depending on digital resources available, and learners could produce computer-generated maps and transform real places on Earth into fantasy lands.

Goals: To understand how setting and place work in science fiction and fantasy, and to practice translating a speculative world and speculative descriptions into a visual form in a map.

Primary Books and Media: *Pastoralia* by George Saunders; *A Wizard of Earthsea* by Ursula K. Le Guin; *A Game of Thrones* or any other book in the A Song of Ice and Fire series by George R. R. Martin; opening sequence of *Game of Thrones*, the HBO television series (https://www.youtube.com/watch?v=s7L2PVdrb_8).

Additional Books and Media: *The Fifth Season* by N. K. Jemisin; *The Magicians* by Lev Grossman; *Perdido Street Station* by China Miéville; *Hild* by Nicola Griffith; *The Coldest Girl in Coldtown* by Holly Black. Many other books have maps included to show where the action is set as well.

Maps are sometimes included in the front or back matter of a work of fiction to give readers a sense of place, and a reference to help follow strange geographies and unfamiliar, invented names. Le Guin's *A Wizard of Earthsea* map shows the intricate, endless islands and archipelago that make up that world. In the final scenes, as the wizard Ged confronts the evil shadow antagonist, an entity Ged himself created with his inexperienced but powerful magic, much of the action takes place on a boat. That map of endless coastline does not literally or scientifically recreate Le Guin's rich geography; in fact, the description in the book is not specific or extensive enough to be recreated in a "scientifically accurate" map. Instead, that map is there to help build the world for the reader, and reinforce the setting in a visual way that lays out the scope and place of the story.

Saunders's *Pastoralia* is a bleak contemporary fantasy where economic downturn means that working on display in a human zoo exhibition—in this case, playing the role of a caveman—is the best job the main character can get. This story does not include a map, but provides fantastic inspiration for participants to imagine one.

Learning Objectives: Participants will

- Examine and study a variety of fictional maps
- Understand how setting contributes to world building in science fiction and fantasy
- Create their own fictional map: either one of their own creation, or by creating a map for the theme park in George Saunders's*Pastoralia*

Duration: 2 hours

Materials Needed:

- Large drawing paper, either from a sketchpad or copier/printer paper, size 11 × 17 (or A3) or larger
- Pencils and erasers

Instructions:

- Show examples from the books in the preceding list. Explain the role maps can play in an SFF work, and ask participants if they know of any examples from books they have read.
- If a computer or device is available, show them the opening sequence of *Game of Thrones*, an animated, clockwork-style representation of the map featured in George R. R. Martin's books.
- Read aloud selections of *Pastoralia*. If there is time, or a sustained series of workshops, have participants read the entire novella.
- Let participants know that there are many fan-created or otherwise unofficial maps and schematics of science-fiction and fantasy worlds for many movies, TV shows, graphic novels, and other media. If there is time and interest, show them the website Fantastic Maps (http://www.fantasticmaps.com/) for more examples.
- Discuss *Pastoralia*: This story details one exhibition in a human zoo or museum. What do you think the rest of the facility looks like? What other time periods are on display? Consider museums and zoos now: What else would be there—a gift shop, a restaurant, or so forth?
- Direct participants to sketch out the plans to this exhibition and zoo/museum/amusement park facility.

- As an alternative or as an additional activity, participants could draw a map or plan from a book or story of their choice, or remake one of the samples in a new way.
- Post these to your library's social media feeds, where appropriate.

Heroes of Feminist Science Fiction Trading Cards

In the golden age of science fiction, women were often decorations and one-dimensional plot devices subject to the gaze of a male hero. As with the rest of American life, the social revolutions that started in the 1950s and continue today affected publishing. While these are by no means the first women who ever wrote science fiction (Mary Shelley's *Frankenstein* is usually considered one of the first SFF texts), Ursula Le Guin, Joanna Russ, and James Tiptree Jr. revolutionized SFF writing at the height of second wave feminism, with complex and provocative work. This program celebrates them.

Goals: To learn about feminist science fiction icons in media and fiction, and create a set of trading cards featuring some of them.

Primary Books and Media: *The Female Man* by Joanna Russ; *The Left Hand of Darkness* by Ursula K. Le Guin; titles by Connie Willis, Octavia Butler, James Tiptree Jr., Lois McMaster Bujold, and Nicola Griffith; *Buffy the Vampire Slayer* (graphic novels and TV show); Aliens movies (*Alien, Aliens, Alien 3, Alien: Resurrection*) with Sigourney Weaver; *The X-Files* (TV show); Star Wars movies (IV: *A New Hope*, V: *The Empire Strikes Back*, VI: *Return of the Jedi*, VII: *The Force Awakens*); *Alias* (TV show); *Supergirl* (TV show); *Agent Carter* (TV show); *Terminator 2* (movie) or *Terminator: The Sarah Connor Chronicles* (TV show).

Additional Books and Media: Graphic novels and other media about female superheroes are an OK substitution, especially for younger participants.

This project covers a lot of ground. SFF by women was published less often in the past than SFF by men.[1] Recent analysis by others demonstrate that although this ratio has improved, the problem has not been resolved.[2] From some of the most prominent women SFF writers of the last 50 years to contemporary feminist icons, this program offers an opportunity to celebrate the contribution of women authors and highlight images of strong women in TV and movies.

The Female Man by Russ concerns a woman, Janet, who arrives from a parallel Earth called Whileaway, where there are no men. Her disorientation at dealing with our gender binary and gender roles provides very effective critiques of these roles. When readers learn about how Whileaway works with only women, they are provoked to think about the roles of women in our world.

Le Guin's *The Left Hand of Darkness* is as groundbreaking a deconstruction of gender as *The Female Man*, but it approaches the theme by dramatizing an alien planet with humans who are just as strange as Janet, in that they are gender neutral, or all of one gender type except when they cycle in and out of being either male or female, depending on all sorts of conditions.

Learning Objectives: Participants will

- Learn about the history of SFF written by women
- Watch and explore the contemporary manifestation of feminist SFF in the guise of iconic female heroes
- Practice designing and arranging a series of trading cards with illustrations and text

Duration: Two 2-hour sessions

Materials Needed:

- Blank index cards (or plain paper folded into quarters)
- Sample trading cards (either ones you have created or any character or sports trading cards)

Instructions:
Session 1

- Show the sample trading cards. Explain that the final product will be cards like this of SFF women heroes.
- Tell the group that even now only about a quarter of SFF books published are by women.[3] Show them books by Joanna Russ, Ursula K. Le Guin, Lois McMaster Bujold, and James Tiptree Jr. (Explain that Tiptree was a pseudonym. See program plan "All about Tiptree: Inventing a Literary Alter Ego.") Read up to a paragraph or two from *The Female Man* or *The Left Hand of Darkness*.
- Ask participants to think about what it must have been to be some of the first women publishing science fiction or fantasy, and what it means to be in the minority.
- Discuss the gender imbalance today in terms of writers and filmmakers: fewer women are writing, directing, and producing movies

than men. Ask them if it influences the way female characters are portrayed.

- Show the rest of the books you have on hand: titles by Nicola Griffith, Octavia Butler, Lois McMaster Bujold, or Connie Willis. Ask participants to think about the book jacket design, and send them into the collection to look for more science fiction and fantasy by women for 10 minutes or so, and also to grab some SFF books by men, too.
- Back together as a group, compare and contrast the books by men and women. Are there any trends in the cover design? Read the blurbs or jacket copy: Are there any trends about what the books are about? Are they about male or female characters? Are any about gay, lesbian, trans, bi, or queer characters?
- End the session with another short passage from *The Female Man*. Encourage participants to check out any of the books you have been discussing, and to come back to the next session thinking about women heroes in TV and movies.

Session 2

- Show clips from the movies and TV shows previously listed. Explain to your participants that you are offering a list of female characters they can use in their trading card sets. They should also feel free to add their own female heroes.
- Challenge participants to create at least eight cards, half with women writers and half with characters from books, TV, or other media.
- They can begin by making their list. For the writers, they should find a short passage from the author's works to put on the card. If computers/printers are available, they should feel free to search for images to use as inspiration or collage.
- Have the group spend the rest of the time making their cards. If they want to, they can trade among themselves at the very end of the program.

NOTES

1. http://feministsf.org/community/history.html
2. http://www.slate.com/blogs/xx_factor/2013/04/25/strange_horizons _report_on_woman_authors_is_science_fiction_and_fantasy.html
3. http://strangehorizons.com/2013/20130422/2sfcount-a.shtml

Vampires from A to V, and Zombies from W to Z: A Lesson in Infographics

Vampires and zombies appear in our mythologies and popular culture over and over again. Probably every teen has seen or read media featuring them, from their original forms (think *Dracula* and *Dawn of the Dead*) through many reinventions (think sparkly daytime vampires in *Twilight* and intelligent zombies in *iZombie*). Because there are so many kinds of each, and they are in constant conversation with each other in books and media, they are ideal subjects for an infographic. Using pictures and design to convey numerical or statistical values is an important twenty-first-century skill, and this program can help teens practice it.

Goals: Learn to read and create infographics, taking a deep dive into vampires and zombies and the different kinds of each that are represented in SF.

Primary Books and Media: *Interview with a Vampire* by Anne Rice; *Buffy the Vampire Slayer* graphic novels; *Fledgling* by Octavia Butler; *30 Days of Night* graphic novels published by IDW Publishing and Pocket Books; *The Walking Dead* graphic novels; *The Strain* by Guillermo del Toro; *The Passage* by Justin Cronin; clips from *28 Days Later* directed by Danny Boyle; *Day of the Dead* or others by George Romero; *iZombie* (TV show); *The Strain* (TV show); selections from *Buffy the Vampire Slayer* season 7, episode 10, "Bring on the Night"; *The Coldest Girl in Coldtown* by Holly Black.

Additional Books and Media: Any other favorite vampire or zombie stories popular among your communities.

Vampires and zombies come in all shapes and sizes. This program gives you an opportunity to show some interesting examples from books and TV/film with very diverse vampires and zombies. Anne Rice's beautiful,

Courtesy of comfreak. https://pixabay.com/en/zombie-horror-undead-monster-bone-367517/.

cunning Lestat is very different from the genetically modified vampire child Shori in Octavia Butler's *Fledgling*. The vampires of del Toro's and Cronin's books would be unrecognizable to Anne Rice's; they are more animal than human, with grotesque physiognomies. Vampire traits that can vary widely include age, how a vampire is created, whether they have telepathy or other powers, whether they can change shape (into a bat or other animal), if they kill to eat, how they can be killed, and so on.

Similarly, *The Walking Dead*'s mindless, relentless monsters who will eat anything move more slowly than the super-fast killing machines in *28 Days Later*. In 2005's *Land of the Dead*, a zombie demonstrates some capacity to think and adapt. In *iZombie* (2015), the main character is a zombie passing as a human and having to hide her brain-eating habit while she solves murders.

Learning Objectives: Participants will

- Compare/contrast traits of vampires across different media
- Compare/contrast traits of zombies across different media
- Examine examples of infographics
- Create an infographic of their own

Duration: 2.5 hours

Materials Needed:

- Whiteboard, scratch paper
- Example infographics, such as
  - "Fastest Ship in the Universe": https://www.fatwallet.com/blog/fastest-ship-in-the-universe/
  - "Prediction or Influence? A History of Books That Forecast the Future": http://www.printerinks.com/images/Admin/Book Predictions_940x3463.jpg
  - Many options on this Pinterest board: https://www.pinterest.com/exploresfmovies/sci-fi-infographics/

Instructions:

- Find samples from the books above that describe the "rules" of vampire or zombie life. Read them, and encourage participants to share any other things about vampires or zombies they know.
- Show clips from the listed TV shows or movies. Some of these images will be scary or disturbing!
- Ask everyone to vote and choose either vampires or zombies. Make the results of this vote into an infographic on the whiteboard.
- Show sample infographics from Internet sources.
- Ask participants to think about how they might represent information about vampires or zombies visually.
  - Comparing their traits in a table
  - Charting their appearance over different TV shows/movies on a timeline
  - Listing or mapping where stories take place
- Individually or in pairs, participants should draft the first iteration of their infographic.
- Circulate among the pairs.
- Bring the group back together and have participants present their first iterations to the group.
- Prompt everyone to ask the following questions:
  - What is the point of the information conveyed?
  - How do the visual aspects enhance the information?
  - What could be more clear?
  - What elements need different or better labels?
- Allow participants to reiterate their designs, and then display them in the library or on social media.

Mock Science Fiction Awards

As this book goes into production, N. K. Jemisin has become the first African-American person to win a Hugo for best novel, and additional Hugos were won by Nigerian-American Nnedi Okorafor for best novella and by Michi Trota for her work on *Uncanny*, making her the first person of Filipino descent to win a Hugo.[1] These 2016 wins happened despite another organized campaign from the Puppies. This program helps teach participants about authors as real people, and about ways in which fan communities reward the books and authors they value.

Goals: To enhance critical thinking skills by learning about two major science fiction and fantasy awards for books, including one chosen by fans, and considering application of awards criteria to books or stories the group is familiar with.

In the past few years, the Hugo Awards have been the source of a controversy in the science fiction and fantasy writer and fan communities. Factions of writers and fans who eventually have become known as the Rabid Puppies and the Sad Puppies organized to protest books and writers they thought were being nominated for and winning Hugo Awards because of a leftist or progressive political agenda. These factions derisively refer to their presumed opponents as SJW or "social justice warriors." The Puppies and others organized slates of candidates for the nominating ballot to counter this "trend," and other writers and fans, in many of the contests in the first year of this protest (2015), chose "no award" instead of awarding a book or author from the "Puppy" slate.[2] You can search for more accounts of this controversy, including fine blog posts from writers such as George R. R. Martin.

Another major literary award, the World Fantasy Award, also experienced recent controversy over the statuette it awards. The statuette was a bust of H. P. Lovecraft, whose racist writings and beliefs became objectionable to the winners being honored with the award, and to the fantasy community it represented.[3] In November 2015, the World Fantasy Award

Courtesy of NASA Ames Research Center. By Rick Guidice. NASA ID Number AC75-1085. http://settlement.arc.nasa.gov/70sArtHiRes/70sArt/art.html.

announced it would replace the statuette after a design competition that would end in September 2016.[4]

Primary Books and Media: *Binti* (a novella) by Nnedi Okorafor (excerpts available for free at http://www.tor.com/2015/08/17/excerpts-binti-nnedi-okorafor/); *Nebula Awards Showcase 2016* edited by Mercedes Lackey; *Nebula Awards Showcase 2015* edited by Matthew Kessel and Greg Bear; *The Long List Anthology: More Stories from the Hugo Awards Nomination List* (The Long List Anthology Series), edited by David Steffen. For the mock ballot, please pull five to seven picture books to use as candidates. This will ensure participants have time to read and consider them all. Suggested titles include: *The Way Back Home* by Oliver Jeffers; *Fossil* by Bill Thomson; *Ice* or *The Giant Seed* by Arthur Geisert; *Boy + Bot* by Ame Dyckman; *The Little Gardener* by Emily Hughes; *Little Night* by Yuyi Morales; *Tar Beach* by Faith Ringgold; Parasite by Mira Grant. Grant—also writing as Seanan McGuire—has received a record number of Hugo nominations in one year.[5]

Additional Books and Media: https://madgeniusclub.com/2016/01/29/hugo-history-a-guest-post-by-ben-yalow/

Learning Objectives: Participants will

- Learn about the major SF awards
- Read samples from winning books and short stories
- Research reviews of the books nominated
- Run a mock ballot for best picture book
- Sketch a design for a new World Fantasy Award

Duration: 2 hours

Materials Needed:

- Printed ballots with the titles and authors names of the picture books up for the "best sci-fi or fantasy picture book" award
- Scrap paper and crayons/markers for sketching
- Access to computers or tablets for researching the titles

Instructions:

- With the group seated in a circle, explain that the Hugo Awards are administered by the World Science Fiction Convention, and that members of that organization are the nominators and voters. This award recognizes excellence in science fiction literature, dividing books and stories into length-based categories (Story, Novelette, Novella, Novel), and including additional awards, including one for TV/film productions. Read more here: http://www.thehugo awards.org/about/.
- Direct participants to find this year's Hugo nominees or more recent winners. Give them 10 minutes of hands-on searching instruction, walking them through how to select a search engine, what query to use, and how to judge which of the top results is likely to be the most authoritative and relevant.
- Return to a circle, and read aloud (or take turns reading aloud) selections from *Binti* by Nnedi Okorafor. Frame this story by telling them it is about a teenager who is running away from home in order to study on a distant planet. No one from her tribe has ever left home, much less Earth. In addition, the people Binti encounters once she leaves have trouble understanding her because of the way she looks. Ask participants to think about any passages they think echo with these themes.
- Ask them what else they liked about this writing: What do they see in it that might have made it award winning? Lead this brief discussion, and prompt them to consider the language used, the richness of description, and the alienness (or not) of the science fiction world Okorafor has created.
- Next, let participants know that they are going to act as awards jury for the next hour. Present them the picture books, one by one. Time permitting, you may read them (or highlight portions of them) with

about 30 seconds of "book talk" content about the book. For simplicity, you can ask them to focus on which they think has the best and most interesting art, the best and most interesting story, and/or the best or most interesting message. For more advanced participants, you might, as a group, come up with other, more formal criteria on which to judge.

- Let participants read and consider the picture book titles. This should be done without discussion.
- Announce a 5-minute warning, and pass out ballots. Participants should vote as quickly as possible, and you should tabulate results.
- The Hugos use instant runoff voting (see http://instantrunoff.com/instant-runoff-home/), so any ties will advance to a runoff.
- Announce the award winner, and discuss. Debrief the participants about the process: How did it feel to compare their votes to others? How did it feel if their choice won or lost?
- Finally, explain the controversy about the Lovecraft statuette detailed above, and challenge participants to design a new award statuette they would be proud to give out and/or win.

NOTES

1. http://www.thehugoawards.org/content/pdf/2016HugoStatistics.pdf
2. http://www.npr.org/2015/08/26/434644645/how-the-sad-puppies-won-by-losing
3. https://www.theguardian.com/books/2015/nov/09/world-fantasy-award-drops-hp-lovecraft-as-prize-image
4. http://www.locusmag.com/News/2016/03/world-fantasy-award-trophy-submissions-update/
5. https://www.theguardian.com/books/2013/mar/31/seanan-mcguire-hugo-awards-shortlist

All about Tiptree: Inventing a Literary Alter Ego

Women publishing with male or gender-neutral names is an old literary practice, but no pseudonym and alter ego was quite like James Tiptree Jr., who not only wrote books and stories but also kept up extended correspondence with other writers in character. The story of Alice Sheldon demonstrates the path of women through science fiction in the twentieth century, and also introduces teen readers to a fascinating mind who lived an extraordinary life.

Goals: To gain understanding of issues surrounding equality in the literary and publishing world through the work of James Tiptree Jr. and to understand the contribution women and feminism made to science fiction, despite significant structural barriers. In addition, participants will be introduced to the concept and some of the reasons behind pseudonyms while inventing their own literary alter ego.

Primary Books and Media: *James Tiptree, Jr.: The Double Life of Alice B. Sheldon* by Julie Phillips; *Letters to Tiptree*, edited by Alexandra Pierce and Alisa Krasnostein.

Additional Books and Media: *How to Suppress Women's Writing* by Joanna Russ.

James Tiptree Jr. was one of the most important science fiction writers of the '50s and '60s, generating highly original worlds and concepts grounded in impeccable hard science. Tiptree was, really, just one of the names under which Alice Sheldon, a writer and former government employee, wrote. Finally, later in her career, she outed herself as "Tiptree." In some ways, Sheldon continued the long tradition evidenced by George Eliot, or the Brontës writing under Currer, Acton, and Ellis Bell, male names that made it easier, presumably, to sell stories and books. A recent experiment confirmed that submissions from men or male names do better than those from women.[1] Sheldon's early life was

Source: https://pixabay.com/en/alien-blaster-defense-futurism-gun-1295093/.

unusual, and as a child, she went on a significant journey to Africa with her adventurer parents. Julie Phillips's biography tells a compelling story. *Letters to Tiptree* features today's most important science fiction and fantasy writers telling Sheldon, in their own words, what her work and her life meant to them.

Learning Objectives: Participants will

- Understand the importance of James Tiptree Jr. as a writer and also as a literary identity in the traditions of science fiction that concerns itself with feminism, the meaning of gender, and sexuality
- Close read a letter to Tiptree
- Invent their own literary alter ego and write a character biography for it

Duration: 1.5 hours

Materials Needed:

- Scrap paper for journaling

Instructions:

- Read a passage from the beginning of the Phillips book, and explain James Tiptree Jr. and Alice Sheldon. Be sure to underline that editors, readers, and other writers did not know Tiptree's "real" identity through most of "his" career.

- Read aloud, or taking turns with participants, letters from the *Letters to Tiptree* anthology. Some recommendations are the letters by: Aliette de Bodard, L. Timmel Duchamp, Nisi Shawl, Brit Mandelo, and Jo Walton.
- Based on the letters, discuss why you think Alice Sheldon decided first to write under a male name, but ultimately to come out as the person behind Tiptree. Although the story is a bit more complicated, as relayed in Phillips, for the purposes of this discussion, participants can assume that she was willing to later be the face of Tiptree.
- Direct participants to think about developing a literary alter ego for themselves. Challenge them to consider an identity that: 1) hides and protects their real identity, 2) gives them supposed authenticity or experience to write a certain kind of book, and 3) frees them to write about anything they would like without anyone they know in real life ever knowing.
- Give them 15 minutes to journal and draft a name, an age and occupation, as well as other biographical details. They can use the author biographies of the above books as models.
- If desired, students can write or type out a clean copy. Pass them all to the middle of the table, and then either read them all aloud, or distribute them for participants to read. As they hear their literary alter egos described, they can chose to identify themselves or not.

NOTE

1. http://jezebel.com/homme-de-plume-what-i-learned-sending-my-novel-out-und-1720637627

Best Book Reviews (with Optional Podcast)

Book reviews are essential professional tools for librarians, and are also the way many people find new books to read. It is important to demonstrate that these are not book reports, and that reviews are meant to demonstrate the teen's own interest in or questions about a book. Teens will practice critical writing skills while promoting or critiquing books they love or hate, and should be encouraged to share their reviews.

Goals: To study the form of a book review and to write a book review. Depending on technology available, participants can also turn their reviews into a book review podcast.

Primary Books and Media: *What Makes This Book So Great* by Jo Walton; any other book reviews chosen from Goodreads.com or other sources.

Additional Books and Media: Classic review clips from Siskel and Ebert (their review of *Star Wars*, 1977, can be found here: https://www.youtube.com/watch?v=Ky9-eIlHzAE).

Reviewing is one of the most powerful tools in the world of writing and books, and amateurs and critics alike can make or break a book with one. An inspiring review should make the book catch and spread like a virus: this is a book you must read! And at the same time, a negative one might turn off potential readers.

Reviewing a book means that a writer has to produce a very brief synopsis that remains meaningful to the writer's analysis and offer an opinion and understanding of the book that gives the book a fair shake. Reviews that contain too much summary are not worth the time; critiques that just tell you they hated it and everything about it are a similar waste. An excellent book review gives a reader an overall impression of the book by conveying specific ideas and examples from the text that illustrate those ideas.

The review, as a form, contains many possibilities, particularly in terms of length and approach. For the sake of time and efficiency in this program, limit participants to 200 or 250 words. (Professional book reviews can run as few as 50 or 100.)

Learning Objectives: Participants will

- Read book reviews and practice the form by writing one
- Write and revise a book review

Duration: 1 hour; podcasting option will take at least 1 additional hour

Materials Needed:

- Paper for writing or computers for composing final drafts of book reviews
- Tablet or smartphone with a podcasting app such as VoiceMemo or Opinion Podcasts—Record, Edit & Share, which is free in the OS App Store

Instructions:

- Explain that the purpose of a book review is to tell readers about a book and give an opinion of the book informed by a careful read. It should not just center on liking or disliking a book, but should instead ask questions about the main characteristics of a book and evaluate how well it achieved its various purposes.
- Read a sample book review. If using the Walton book, read/distribute copies of her essays about Octavia Butler or Maureen McHugh.
- Ask participants to discuss what worked well and what did not in the review: Was there enough detail about the story? Is the reviewer's point of view and tone clear? Did the reviewer like or enjoy the book? How can you tell? Prompt them to offer textual evidence from the review in this discussion, so they are close reading.
- Direct them to make a short list of two or three books they have recently read. Direct them to search for reader reviews of those books on Goodreads.com. After 15 minutes or so, gather the participants back together to ask them what they found. Use similar questions as above: Did the reviewer enjoy the book? Did the reviewer give enough story, too much, or not enough? What did you like about the review? Since it is a book you have also read, what did you think of the review? Do you agree? What would you add? Did this review make you reconsider any ideas or opinions you had of the book previously?
- Then direct them to review a book on their own. It will help if they have access to the book, so build in time for them to find a copy on your shelves, if available. Remind them they should use specific examples and passages from the books they are reviewing. They should aim for 200 words maximum length.

- Time permitting, read and revise the book reviews in pairs using a peer review model.
- If desired, encourage participants to publish these reviews to Goodreads.com, or on the library's blog or social media, where appropriate.
- If desired, edit a clean copy of the review for broadcast, and direct the participant to read it aloud a few times, practicing for clarity, fluid speech, and intelligibility. Then record them via a podcast app, and post/share as appropriate.

Short Story Trailer

With the advent on easy online video streaming, short trailer videos have emerged as a marketing technique for writers and publishers. They use video, pictures, sound, titles (captions), and narration to attract readers and creative positive attention for their stories or books. This program lets participants practice basic slideshow techniques to approximate a trailer, and works great as a follow-up program to "Best Book Reviews." The China Miéville story suggested below is an excellent model for a script for a movie trailer.

Goals: To learn writing, editing, and cinematography skills by adapting a short story into a visual format and using simple videography techniques —photography and editing—while transforming a story into a promotional trailer.

Primary Books and Media: "Bloodchild" in *Bloodchild and Other Stories* by Octavia Butler; *Yellowcake* by Margo Lanagan. The Children's Book Council has an expansion YouTube channel of YA book trailers located here: https://www.youtube.com/playlist?list=PLF5316EC25DD56E15.

Additional Books and Media: Selections from *Three Moments of an Explosion* by China Miéville, including "The Crawl"; "Singing My Sister Down" by Margo Lanagan in *Black Juice*.

Learning Objectives: Participants will

- Read a short story and identify its main ideas and most attractive qualities
- Storyboard a trailer promoting the story based on these main ideas and themes
- Film and edit a short story trailer

Duration: Three 1.5-hour workshops over 3 days

Materials Needed:

- Tablet or smartphone with video or video editing app such as iMovie or YouTube Capture; if there is no technological infrastructure, students should create instead a storyboard for this trailer as though they were planning to film and produce it. *Note:* Depending on the app chosen, there might be different functionality in terms of editing, splicing in still frames, or using text and titles. Pick an app that you and your users can master relatively quickly, so more time is spent developing out the idea and narration for the trailer. Or, schedule an extra practice session for perfecting their in-app editing skills.

Instructions:

First Workshop

- Show sample book trailers from the link listed above, or others you have identified based on the interests of your participants.
- Tell participants that they will, over this and two additional workshop sessions, read a short story, plan and design a storyboard for a trailer promoting that short story, and then use a tablet or smartphone to film it.
- Read the China Miéville story "Crawl," which is a fictional experiment in the form of a script/shot-by-shot description of a movie trailer. Read it through twice, prompting participants to think about the words and description and how a director might translate that into images.
- Ask them to sketch out some storyboard concepts as you read "Crawl" a second or third time. How is Miéville playing with and testing out the limits of translating "movie trailer" language into text? How does this story embrace and play with tropes and patterns they recognize from film trailers they usually see?
- Direct them to find additional book trailers with online searches: "rick riordan book trailer," for example, or other Google queries. They should spend 15 minutes or so finding and viewing additional book trailers.
- Bring the participants back together and distribute copies of "Bloodchild." Tell them a basic frame for the story: it's from the point of view of a human child living on an alien world, in a protected reserve at the mercy of an alien species called the Tlic. Depending on copies available, begin reading the short story together.

Second Workshop

- Continue reading "Bloodchild." If participants have read it themselves in the time between workshops, isolate key passages and close read them together: what happens to Bram Lomas, what happens to Gan at the end of the story. Answer questions and discuss how they understand the action of the story.

- Prompt the group to reread, flagging or underlining any key images or descriptive language in Butler's story that will translate immediately to a visual. T'Gatoi's body is an excellent example, as is how Butler describes her style of moving.
- Distribute storyboard templates. Depending on available tablet resources, this might work better in pairs or in groups of three.
- Challenge them to boil down "Bloodchild" to a minute of narration. Participants then outline this narration, and time themselves reading it aloud to be sure they are within time limits. Remind them of the effective examples they have seen in the first workshop that balance narration with pauses, silences, sound effects, and use of music.
- Next, they begin to storyboard the 60 seconds of trailer visuals by sketching the visual they intend to accompany the narration.
- Let them work on this for 20 minutes or more. End the session by reminding them of Miéville's "Crawl" and how it describes each shot in a trailer.
- Tell the group they will return to this storyboard and finalize it at the next workshop, and that they can work on it in the meantime, and may want to gather prompts or still images they will use in their trailer.

Third Workshop

- Prepare the tablets or smartphones with video apps. Depending on available technology, participants may want to include special effects.
- Give them 15 minutes to search for still images via Google image search to download and add to their projects. Give them a copyright disclosure, and let them know they are doing this for practice and to prove their skills, and that they should not post or share these if they contain images that the participants or the library does not have permission to use or publish.
- With final images in hand, direct the workshop participants to take an additional 15 minutes to finalize and revise their storyboards.
- Let the pairs or groups of three spend the rest of the workshop filming, editing, and revising their trailers. Take the last 10 minutes of the program to show everyone's work in progress. Schedule an additional workshop session—or extend this one—to show more finished works, if you like.

SFF Readers' Theater

Readers' theater is a trusted way of getting even the shyest participants up in front of you and their peers. It helps them with reading aloud, and reading more fluently, and helps them build cooperation with each other in a playful and theatrical way. Readers' theater works with a variety of age groups in many different settings. The stories suggested here are complex and appropriate for older teens. With much younger participants, consider adapting something more familiar, such as a folk tale or urban legend.

Goals: To enhance writing, editing, and performance skills by creating a readers' theater play out of a short story and performing the short story for a library audience.

Primary Books and Media: "Amnesty" by Octavia Butler in *Bloodchild and Other Stories*; "Singing My Sister Down" by Margo Lanagan in *Black Juice*.

Additional Books and Media: Additional instructor resources are available here: http://www.readingrockets.org/article/readers-theater-giving-students-reason-read-aloud.

Readers' theater could be described as a souped-up read-aloud where participants take the roles and deliver the key dialogue and narration of a story in a group performance. In this program, students can reflect on point of view, narrative voice, setting, and detail, all fictional elements that need special consideration in readers' theater. They will also focus on the dialogue, carefully and closely reading for the most crucial conversations and the most crucial moments.

Learning Objectives: Participants will

- Understand the role of dialogue in fiction
- Isolate dialogue and its role in characterization
- Transform a short story into a readers' theater script
- Perform, if desired, a staged reading of their script

Duration: 2–3 hours

Materials Needed:

- Highlighters
- Markable copies of the story; a copy of the story that can be cut up and rearranged would also be useful

Instructions:

- Explain that readers' theater is a group reading exercise that is more than just reading aloud and less than a fully staged play. It is more like a radio play, in that it uses dialogue and essential narration to move the story along without containing any visual information: sets, actions, props, and so forth.
- Read the story aloud. Ask participants to mark the most interesting or compelling parts in highlighter as you read.
- Together (using a whiteboard or butcher paper, if available) make a list of any characters and whether they have speaking parts.
- Now hone in on the highlighted sections. If any of them are in dialogue already in the story, note it, but be especially concerned with interesting and compelling parts of the story that are in narration rather than in dialogue. How can this be handled in a play or performance? Present this problem to your group, and suggest that you solve it by creating a narrator character who can help fill in the details and blanks in between bits of dialogue.
- Have participants do an abbreviated group read-through with just the most important narrative and the speaking parts. How does it sound? Is the meaning coming through? Are there places where the dialogue needs more description, qualification, or accompanying action?
- Rearrange (by cutting and pasting, or by retyping) all of the out-loud parts of the story: this is your readers' theater script. Refine the script again, and then practice reading it aloud as a group.
- Refine and perform this short story as appropriate.

Best Adapted Screenplay

Some of your teens might be aspiring screenwriters, and surely many of them are movie fans. Showing them what a screenplay looks like opens up their critical understanding of how media is produced and at what stage the writer has the most impact. In addition, this program teaches them about Asimov's laws of robotics, one of the most famous thought experiments in science fiction, and has a great, contemporary tie-in with a Will Smith movie.

Goals: To learn about screenplay format and visual language by translating a page of text or narrative into images.

Primary Books and Media: *I, Robot: The Illustrated Screenplay* by Isaac Asimov and Harlan Ellison; *I, Robot* by Isaac Asimov; *I, Robot* (2004 film).

Additional Books and Media: Any other book/movie combination will also work for this program. Good examples are Andy Weir's *The Martian* and the film adaptation of *The Martian* (2015); in addition, you could use a TV show such as *Game of Thrones* (HBO) and the George R. R. Martin novels it is based on (with a strong content warning for younger participants!); or *11/22/63* (Hulu) and the Stephen King novel it is based on. Any other adaptation of a science fiction or fantasy novel can be substituted in. The Asimov texts are excellent because participants will have 1) the narrative fiction example, 2) Ellison's screenplay version, and 3) the film to watch and compare.

The key to this program is to isolate several sections of the narrative to compare to the corresponding sections in the screenplay and the movie. Tell participants that one page of screenplay is about a minute on film; as a result, whatever section you isolate to work on should be just two or three pages of screenplay and a movie clip just a few minutes long.

Learning Objectives: Participants will

- Learn the basics of screenplay format
- Read selections from Asimov's classic robot stories

                    JOHN
          Well, one can't have everything.

                                             CUT TO:

EXT. JOHN AND MARY'S HOUSE - CONTINUOUS

An old car pulls up to the curb and a few KNOCKS as the
engine shuts down.

MIKE steps out of the car and walks up to the front door. He
rings the doorbell.

                                             BACK TO:

INT. KITCHEN - CONTINUOUS

                    JOHN
          Who on Earth could that be?

                    MARY
          I'll go and see.

Mary gets up and walks out.

The front door lock CLICKS and door CREAKS a little as it's
opened.

                    MARY (O.S.) (CONT'D)
          Well hello Mike! Come on in! John,
          Mike's here!

                    JOHN
          Hiya Mike! What brings you here?

Mary walks in, Mike following. Both sit down at the kitchen
table, opposite one another.

                    MIKE
          Oh, just thought I'd bring back
          your revolver. Thanks for letting
          me borrow it last week.

Mike reaches in his pocket and fishes out a hammerless Smith
& Wesson. He opens the cylinder with a CLICK and confirms
it's unloaded before setting it on the table.

John removes the paper towel from his plate, setting the
bacon down on it. Then he takes his sunny-side up eggs from
the frying pan and puts them on the plate. He sits down
between Mike and Mary.

Source: https://commons.wikimedia.org/wiki/File:Screenplay_example.svg.

Duration: Depending on the age of the participants and the time available, this program could last for several workshop sessions. At the minimum, participants will need 2 hours to read the selections, discuss the format, watch the video clips, and produce a page or two of screenplay. If desired, groups could elect to read the entire story or stories, watch the whole movie, and produce more pages of screenplay adaptation.

Materials Needed:

- Copies of a page of screenplay (can be from Ellison, above), or any samples found online
- The software program Final Draft, designed for screenwriting professionals, has a handy guide to formatting screenplays: http://www.finaldraft.com/mm_media/mm_pdf/How_to_Format_a_Screenplay.pdf. Here is another sample with more definitions: http://www.storysense.com/format/margins.htm.

Instructions:

- Distribute screenplay sample pages, and walk participants through the formatting:
  - "FADE IN" and other camera/visual instructions in capital letters
  - Scene headings that show whether shots are interior or exterior, and where they are taking place
  - "Slug lines" that demonstrate the important action taking place in the scene
  - Dialogue marked by centered name tags
  - Action described left-justified, outside of the dialogue
  - O.S. means "off screen," and so forth
- Isolate a few pages of Asimov's short story and its corresponding screenplay version. Close read the two side by side as a group, noticing which actions and pieces of dialogue were literally cut from one and pasted into the other. Zoom in on any differences, variations, or liberties taken with the source material: Where is it different? Why is it different between the visual and print media? Is that the choice you might have made?
- If possible, queue up clips of the same sequence from *I, Robot*, the movie. Prompt them to compare and contrast first the screenplay sequence and the film clip: How did the words translate into camera movements, directions, special effects, characterizations, and so forth? Secondarily, compare the clip to the original short story text: How are the themes the same or different? Is the style, tone, or feeling different? Why and how?
- Return to a new sequence in the Asimov text. As a group, write the scene heading and slug line, and then begin chunking the action and dialogue on the short story page into screenplay format. After

several minutes of practice, you can transition to participants working on the translation themselves.

- Let them work for 15 minutes or more, then gather together again to compare their screenplays to the Ellison sample. Point out and praise any places where the screenplays are similar, and do the same where they differ. Ask these new screenwriters why they made the choices they did, and what they think of Ellison's version. How else could they refine their "translation"?
- Watch the corresponding clip from the movie, and compare and contrast differences.
- At this point, participants can continue retranslating *I, Robot*, or they could apply their new screenplay skills to another short story and begin adapting it.

Piracy and Ownership: From Copyright to Creative Commons

When engaging in fan culture and Internet remix culture, where memes rule and fans share clips, reedits, redubs, and even their own fan fictions that send characters in all sorts of unauthorized directions, fans should be aware of how copyright might apply to them. As budding creators of intellectual property (both in the course of these programs and in their other projects), these teens should learn about Creative Commons rights, when they can use the work of others in their own work, and when and how they might make their work available for others to respond to, remix, and use.

Goals: To learn how copyright law applies to books and media, and understand the limits of copyright and how to use Creative Commons licenses.

Primary Books and Media: Cory Doctorow, *Information Doesn't Want to Be Free*; this article as a primer: http://www.locusmag.com/Perspectives/2015/01/cory-doctorow-a-new-deal-for-copyright/; Cory Doctorow, *Little Brother* or *Pirate Cinema*; it is useful to have some YouTube clips to show to understand "take-down" notices. This blog is also provocative and accessible on the topic: http://www.sarahmadisonfiction.com/2016/06/dear-broke-reader-your-sense-of-entitlement-is-killing-me/.

THE DIGITAL MILLENNIUM COPYRIGHT ACT (DMCA)

While there are many sites where users can illegally access (via download) almost any content they desire, from Hollywood blockbuster movies to e-books and whole albums, most of the legal ways of accessing music and video content cost. They cost in part because the Digital Millennium Copyright Act (DMCA) makes it necessary to pay the copyright holders for accessed materials. This often means that when a user buys a song from iTunes or the Google Play stores, or an e-book from Amazon, the files have a built-in Digital Rights Management (DRM), which locks down the file and makes it hard or impossible to copy, modify, or share more widely.

DMCA and DRM are very controversial topics, with copyright holders and production companies trying to protect profits on the one hand, and a somewhat radical philosophy of open and free access to all information, all the time, on the other. Most Internet users will find themselves in the middle of these two camps, so it is necessary to educate them about the legality of sharing music and videos online. It is also worthwhile to introduce the other side of the argument, for free and open access.

CREATIVE COMMONS LICENSES

In response to closed copyright, a movement to offer licensed content that users can download for free, remix and adulterate, as well as share more widely themselves has sprung up: Creative Commons. This is a kind of copyright license that lets content creators stipulate exactly what users can do with their content (text, photographs, music, or video) for free and without asking permission. These licenses are a great way to learn about fair use and other copyright issues. Their mission is to build an infrastructure of content and rules for that content in order to maximize users' potential to creatively engage and share with other artistic and creative endeavors. The website has an easy-to-use tool that helps users choose a license. Users must decide, for example, if they will let others modify their work in anyway, and if they will allow any commercial use of their work. It also stipulates very clearly how the work should be attributed to the creator to help make sure others are not passing off someone else's work as their own.

Learning Objectives: Participants will

- Understand the limits of fair use and the Digital Millennium Copyright Act
- Understand how Creative Commons licenses work
- Know how to use the Electronic Frontier Foundation (https://www.eff.org/) as a resource

Duration: 2 hours

Materials Needed:

- A computer or tablet for accessing the Creative Commons site, as well as YouTube or other streaming video sites, such as Vimeo

Source: https://pixabay.com/en/comic-book-marvel-books-shop-1393153/.

Instructions:

- Explain that copyright is a way the law guarantees creators access to and control of their intellectual property in the way of stories, pictures, ideas, and so forth.
- Demonstrate several searches for protected material on free video sites such as YouTube. Have them practice searching for their favorite songs, TV shows, and so on. Ask them to notice:
  - How long the clips are—do they show the whole movie or show?
  - Is there additional music added in over the audio track of the video?
  - Do any of the videos feature disclaimers such as "I do not claim to own this material"?
  - Did participants encounter notices saying that the content had been taken down because of copyright violation?
- Explain that copyright holders and producers (especially large media production and distribution companies) use algorithms, that is, pieces of computer code that automatically search out and block protected material.[1]
- Read passages from *Pirate Cinema* aloud, particularly the details of the kids cutting together their pirate films near the end.
- Discuss how Doctorow has heightened the realities of our electronic surveillance in ways that are even scarier because the structures he describes already exist and govern lives in the United Kingdom, elsewhere in Europe, and in North America, too.

- Define plagiarism in the context of copyright infringement. Make the distinction that the former is about who created the idea/image/intellectual content while the latter is about who owns and controls the right to make profit from the idea/image/content.
- Some participants may feel hopeless and frustrated by copyright at this point. Explain to them that Creative Commons licenses are one way artists and writers are able to take control of their content and make it available to wider audiences, or even to voluntary remixing. Point them to the descriptions of the licenses here: https://creativecommons.org/licenses/. When they have read and briefly discussed these licenses, ask them which kind of license they might use to release their own intellectual property, and why.
- Continue the discussion by flipping the question: point participants to this Creative Commons search engine (https://search.creative commons.org/) and ask them to find images or other material they might want to use as their logo, or in a creative project. What do they notice about the types of licenses available and how they can be used?

NOTE

1. https://www.wired.com/2012/09/streaming-videos-robotic-overlords-algorithmic-copyright-cops/

Graphic Novel Point/Counterpoint

Graphic novels continue to attract diverse readership from young adults and other audiences, and are a medium that might attract nontraditional or reluctant readers. This program tasks teens with careful close reading and study of text and images compared to video clips in a medium that can be motivating to them.

Goals: To better understand the process of TV and film adaptations of graphic novels and comics. And to learn how the adapters make choices about translating the images and story.

Primary Books and Media: For younger participants, use any graphic novels from the *Avatar: The Last Airbender* series; for older audiences, consider the following series: *The Walking Dead, 30 Days of Night, Snowpiercer,* or Alan Moore's standalone *Watchmen*; M. Night Shyamalan's *The Last Airbender* (2010); *The Walking Dead* (TV series), David Slade's *30 Days of Night* (2007), Bong Joon-ho's *Snowpiercer* (2013), or Zach Snyder's *Watchmen* (2009); *Nathan Hale's Hazardous Tales: Treaties, Trenches, Mud, and Blood: A World War I Tale* by Nathan Hale.

Additional Books and Media: Any book based on a superhero character (Wonder Woman, Superman, Spider-Man, etc.) where you can find comic or graphic novel adaptations or film or cartoon adaptations (the latter is especially recommended when you're working with younger audiences).

No matter which graphic novel and film/TV show you've chosen, isolate just a few pages and corresponding clips. For most of the texts with adult content that are mentioned in the preceding lists, there are plenty of sequences that avoid graphically sexual or violent content.

Learning Objectives: Participants will

- Read and examine popular graphic novels and their film or TV adaptations

- Learn how images and visual language translate from print to moving image formats

Duration: At least 2 hours. Longer explorations of any given comics/film comparison could fill many more workshop hours.

Materials Needed:

- Computer or tablet for TV/movie clips

Instructions:

- This program involves a lot of close reading, so you will need multiple copies, reproductions, or small groups of participants working together.
- If participants are unfamiliar with the source material, give them a brief (a few minutes max) summary of the world, characters, or story for reference. Then, distribute the panels and describe the flow of action in them. Reading comics aloud needs to balance the dialogue with describing the kinetic action in the pictures without breaking the overall narrative flow. If there is time, reading an entire issue of a comic (as comics tend to be relatively short) will match up better with the video clip.
- Queue up the corresponding segments of the TV or movie adaptation. If they are exact matches to the frames, play them twice. If it is a more general match in terms of characters, settings, and action portrayed but not exactly the frames, once will do.
- Prompt the participants to discuss the two versions, asking them what they noticed in both media, and what elements were limited to just the graphic novel or the film/TV version.
- On butcher paper or a whiteboard, draw a large Venn diagram to represent these categories, and begin filling them in. Asking reluctant speakers to serve as note takers is an excellent way to engage them.
- After 20 minutes or so, review the list and then watch more clips and read more panels, if they are interested in uncovering more similarities and differences to compare and contrast.
- Conclude by directing them, as experts in graphic novel adaptations, to write a letter to fans of the comic recommending whether or not they should watch the film version. They should use at least five examples from the discussion in their letters. If desired, have them exchange letters with a workshop partner, who can read it and give them feedback.

Board Game Adaptation

One of the classic board games of geek culture, Settlers of Catan, features a constantly changing landscape with variable resources. Versions of it with themes from SFF, such as Star Trek Catan, have appeared as well, and there has also been a spin-off novel. This program is in conversation with "Strange Maps," and could be an activity that you play in your library again and again. Your teens are creative geniuses, so please share anything they make. (On Twitter: @joelanichols.)

Goals: To create a board game based on a popular science fiction or fantasy novel.

Primary Books and Media: *Wolf by Wolf* by Ryan Graudin; *The Hunger Games* by Suzanne Collins; *Leviathan Wakes* by James S. A. Corey; clips from the Hunger Games movie series, or from the television series *The Expanse*, based on the James S. A. Corey series; *Barbarian Lord* by Matt Smith.

Additional Books and Media: Many books or media already feature board game adaptations, including the Star Trek franchises, *Game of Thrones, Dune, Harry Potter,* and others. It may be useful to offer examples to participants from BoardGameGeek.com, a site which features information about and user-submitted photographs of thousands of board games, such as: https://boardgamegeek.com/boardgame/121/dune.

Learning Objectives: Participants will

- Learn how to translate the main ideas of a science fiction novel or story into a board game
- Learn how the central conflict of the story drives these stories, and how it could create an engaging game

Duration: Three to four 1.5-hour-long sessions. This duration can vary depending on the complexity, completeness, and playability of the games produced.

Source: https://pixabay.com/en/board-game-play-strategy-fun-933165/.

Materials Needed:

- A board game to play: any genre game you prefer, or a strategy game like Settlers of Catan
- Cardboard, construction paper, scissors, index cards, markers, and rulers
- In addition, any small toys or objects that can be used to identify players (think of the tokens or pieces in Monopoly, like the top hat or thimble). These can be temporarily repurposed from other games, or collected. Feel free to use supplies such as paper clips, binder clips, coins, stones, or beads. Challenge participants to forage for likely items in between sessions 1 and 2.

Instructions:

First Workshop

- Show examples of SFF board games. Use actual games, if available. If not, use images from the above links on a tablet or in color printout.
- Play a board game. Whether Monopoly, Sorry, or something like Settlers of Catan, play several rounds slowly and with lots of discussion and explanation.
- Ask participants to jot down notes about:

Source: https://pixabay.com/en/board-game-competition-strategy-761586/.

- • What makes the game move—how does it move the action from player to player?
  - • What makes the game fun? What makes it frustrating?
  - • How do you win? What are the strategies to win? What are the "wild cards" or other sources of conflict for the players?
- End this session by reading aloud passages from *The Hunger Games*, particularly ones describing the geographies of the districts or of the Hunger Games arena. Direct participants to close their eyes as they listen, and to sketch out (with eyes closed) any ideas or images they picture.
- Share their sketches, and prompt them to think about how they are going to construct the game board in the next session.

Second Workshop

- Review sketches. Pass out large squares of cardboard and crayons and pencils. These are draft game boards.
- Prompt participants, individually or in pairs, to plan a physical layout for their game board. They can focus on colors and specific images at a later phase. In this iteration, have them focus on translating the setting into the game board, and also begin plotting out how the players (or their tokens) will move and advance both physically around the board, but also advance and win the game.

- Prompt them to sketch an action walkthrough, with arrows showing the path to victory.
- Put aside the draft sketches, and return to passages from *The Hunger Games*. Ask them to notice and note the sources of conflict. Moderate up to 10 minutes discussing and describing the sources of conflict, and prompt them to imagine how this conflict will materialize in their game. Consider: Is the central conflict between the players of the game? Between the players on the one hand, and the rules of the game itself? A mixture of the two? What are the best ways to make Suzanne Collins's conflicts real, in the game, and interesting and challenging to players?
- In pairs or groups of up to four, participants should coalesce around a list of rules and a series of objectives for their games. These can follow the format of:
  - Objectives: players need to achieve X in order to advance levels; Y levels means they win the game.
  - Rules: players have to do this; players may do this; when this happens in the game (e.g., someone rolls a 7), this other thing happens.

Third Workshop

- Review the rules and central conflicts of the games being developed. Review the sketches and suggested game play.
- Distribute new blank game boards. Prompt participants to begin matching their rules and objectives with physical game space and the direction/action of the game play.
- Ask them to finalize their game board designs with collage, drawing with markers, and so forth, and to choose the tokens or other objects that will play a role in the game.
- As they iterate a more complete draft of the game, each group should team up with another group and walk each other (in turn) through the new game, with a sample round or two to help identify glitches and iron out bugs.
- Direct the groups to keep working and test playing each other's games.

Fourth Workshop

- Allow 25 minutes to finalize the games, and then present them to the entire group. Spend as much time as participants want playing these games in the library.
- If desired, ask them to write manuals documenting their game's rules, and consider keeping the games available for play in the library.

Spaceship Comparison Cards

Card games and trading cards are another staple of geek culture, and this program tasks teens with flexing their critical thinking skills about spaceships. They have to consider what characteristics of a ship are most desirable, and how the ships from their favorite media stack up. In addition, they can trade these cards with each other or play a card game with them as soon as they have finished making them.

Goals: To learn research and comparison skills by exploring fictional spaceship designs, and to generate interest in reading about them.

Primary Books and Media: *Spaceships: An Illustrated History of the Real and the Imagined* by Ron Miller; *Blast: Spaceship Sketches and Renderings* by Scott Robertson; interactive infographic at http://www.popularmechanics. com/space/deep-space/a18454/sci-fi-starship-size-visualization/; spaceship comparison infographics in *Sci-Fi Chronicles*, edited by Guy Haley.

Learning Objectives: Participants will

- Practice research and comparison skills
- Practice designing and arranging a series of trading cards with illustrations and text
- Invent an impromptu game with their cards

Duration: Two 2-hour sessions

Materials Needed:

- Access to computers or tablets for researching spaceships specs. Access to a printer, if you would like the participants to print out images of their ships; if not, encourage them to sketch their ideas. Some participants may be reluctant to draw them, but remind them that these will become their own trading cards, so they should consider "branding" them as their own, or in a consistent style.

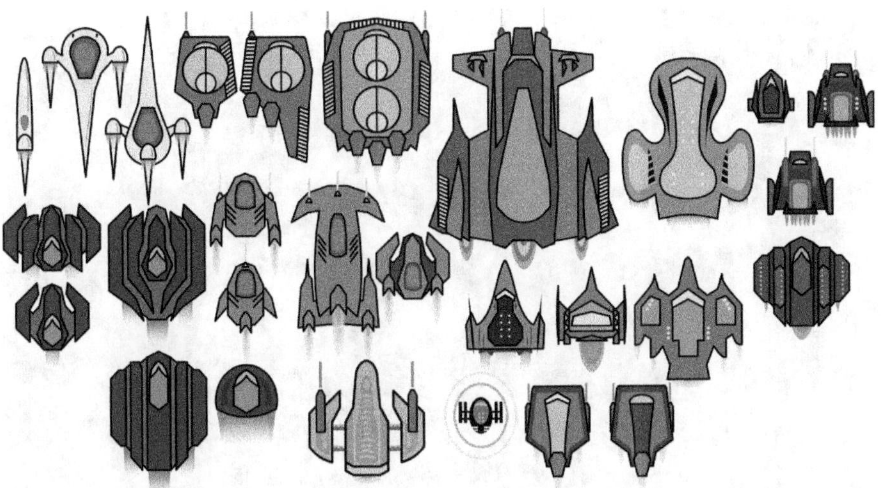

Source: https://pixabay.com/en/video-laser-alien-game-space-ship-38239/.

- Plain paper folded in quarters or blank index cards; sample trading cards (either ones you have created or any character or sports trading cards)

Instructions:

First Workshop

- Explain that participants will pick 5–10 different spaceships to research and report on in trading card form.
- Prompt them with a list of ships from the sources above, and let them browse these materials. In addition, guide them to search for more information online.
- Let them know that each card should contain some basic data that is comparable across all or most ships, such as mass, length, top speed, and number of crew.
- Tell participants to choose which indicators they will feature on each card.
- Prompt them to draw and hand letter their cards. (If necessary and there is computer and printer access, they could print images and text to collage.)
- Have the group use the rest of time to research the comparison indicators and practice drawing their ships.

Second Workshop

- Return to the examples from the books and websites above. Let participants know that they will be sharing and comparing these cards,

Source: https://pixabay.com/en/cape-canaveral-usa-space-center-992547/.

and they should be clear, concise, and reflect each participant's individual style.

- Let them finalize their cards for 45 minutes. Anyone who finishes early can work on adding additional cards to the deck.
- In the last hour, gather the group in a circle and let each person present one card. Prompt them to share and trade their cards. If desired, prompt them to invent their own games with them. For example, shuffle them upside down and then flip them over; spaceship with fastest speed or smallest size or time travel capability wins.

Simple Special Effects

Fan films are a testament to the fact that very sophisticated special effects can be created on tablets and home computers, although of course the software and equipment do still require substantial cost, especially at the commercial or Hollywood level. Teens should think critically about the images and media they consume, and considering how special effects make the unreal visually real is an interesting way for them to begin that understanding. Teens will love the confidence boost from manipulating a lightsaber onto a photo or video of themselves, too.

Goals: To understand how digital special effects can be created, and to practice creating them with an app.

Primary Books and Media: Clips featuring target special effects; here, for example, is a special effects reel from *Star Wars: The Force Awakens*: http://www.slate.com/blogs/browbeat/2016/01/15/star_wars_the_force_awakens_vfx_reel_shows_how_new_worlds_are_made_and_destroyed.html. It is noteworthy because it shows the before/after footage.

Learning Objectives: Participants will

- Learn how to add basic special effects to videos
- Practice basic video editing techniques

Duration: 2 hours

Materials Needed:

- Tablets with special effects apps, such as Lens Distortions, FxGuru, ClonErase, Matter, Saber Movie FX, or iMovie. Check the app store for the latest prices, but at print, the costliest were $4.99, and many were free or $1.99.
- Additional movie-making tips for kids here: http://www.mini moviemakers.com/

Instructions:

- The point-and-click specifics of this program will vary widely depending on the technology and apps available. Libraries with video studios and/or green screens will be able to engage in these techniques more deeply than a single librarian equipped with a smartphone.
- With some expensive software, such as Adobe After Effects, the variety of effects available is impressive and professional-looking. Free apps might only have one or two filters or effects. In a pinch, you can run this program with any photo app with filters, even something like Snapchat, with its stickers and face swapping.
- Demonstrate the capability of the apps on hand by showing samples.
- Show YouTube clips of lightsaber duels, space battles, magic effects, and so forth.
- Ask participants to brainstorm or storyboard what effects they want to create.
- Experiment and iterate with the effects available in your software.
- Share and post to the library's social media.

Monsters of Makeup

From cosplay to Halloween costumes to a popular reality show, monster and creature makeup is a fun and important part of fandom and geek culture. Convention-goers attend as their favorite characters, and invent and interpret those characters physically. Makeup can be silly or truly frightening, and the expert tutorials you will watch in this program will entertain your teens and inspire them.

Goals: To learn about and practice makeup and character makeup techniques.

Primary Books and Media: *Extreme Costume Makeup: 25 Creepy & Cool Step-by-Step Demos* by Brian and Nick Wolfe; *A Complete Guide to Special Effects Makeup* by Tokyo SFX Makeup Workshop; *Face Off* (TV show).

Additional Books and Media: YouTube makeup tutorials like these:
https://www.youtube.com/watch?v=lp5umcDENno
https://www.youtube.com/watch?v=IX7K50SyE8M

And many others from the SFX Makeup Channel YouTube channel available here: https://www.youtube.com/channel/UCGKhKj4FHfhDuPvvxMbyKwQ

Learning Objectives: Participants will

- Understand the basics of creating character makeup
- Be exposed to makeup and hair art as careers
- Practice with designing and applying makeup

Duration: 2 hours

Materials Needed:

- Papier-mâché masks (if made in advance by participants) or blank craft masks like these: http://www.joann.com/mask-it-full-mask/5714522.html
- Tablet or computer for accessing TV clips and tutorials

Source: https://pixabay.com/en/hans-boodt-mannequin-faces-mask-1006031/.

- Makeup to experiment with. This can be any varieties of lipstick, eyeshadows, and so on, and can also be Halloween face paint kits that are widely available. If not using masks, participants could paint on their own faces as desired.
- Baby wipes and paper towels for cleanup

Instructions:

- Show clips from *Face Off*, and at least one YouTube tutorial.
- Structure this program like an episode of *Face Off*, where you issue a creative challenge to the participants. Themes as broad as "villain," "inspired by an animal," or "alien creature" will suffice, and have recurred on this show many times.
- Start with sketches of the makeup concept. Circulate among the participants and help them clarify their idea by identifying additional reference images and/or makeup tutorials. Let them spend 30 minutes or more researching additional resources and sketching.
- Unleash the makeup. It will be messy and hilarious. Some of the participants may really surprise you. Have plenty of paper towels and baby wipes available. Take pictures and post and share as appropriate.

Gagh, Soylent Green, and ChickieNobs: When SF Makes Food Disgusting

Teens are often hungry, and food programs usually attract a vigorous crowd. SFF food might delight and disgust in equal measure, though, as the point of this program is to delve into the ways creators use food to build worlds, distinguish an alien species, or create difference in a given world. You can judge your crowd and make this as gross-out or as palatable as they are.

Goals: To understand how fictional food functions as setting and world building, and how writers and directors characterize science fiction and fantasy creatures, beings, and aliens with the foods they eat and their culinary customs.

Primary Books and Media: *Archivist Wasp* by Nicole Kornher-Stace; *Oryx and Crake* by Margaret Atwood; clips from *Star Trek: The Next Generation*; clip from *Soylent Green.*

Learning Objectives: Participants will

- Research science-fiction recipes
- Taste-test an "unusual food," if desired

Duration: 1 hour

Materials Needed:

- Tablet or computer for viewing clips
- Edible insect candy (if desired); durian fruit (if desired)

Instructions:

- Read passages from the beginning of *Oryx and Crake*, particularly the ones that describe ChickieNobs and pigoons.

- Watch clips of Klingons eating from the Star Trek franchise, such as: https://www.youtube.com/watch?v=tSNVQL8nImU.
- Review this gross Mashable list covering similar ungustables from other movies and worlds: http://mashable.com/2015/06/04/gross-sci-fi-food/.
- Ask participants to react with one word in a round robin format. The one word should describe these foods. Do several of these rounds until you have noted a long list of colorful adjectives.
- Guide users through Internet searches to find recipes for one or more of these foods.
- End the program by asking participants to share the weirdest thing they have ever eaten, and/or invite them to try unusual food such as edible insects, insect candy, durian fruit, and so forth.
- If desired, prompt the group to extend this activity to writing their own recipe for a sci-fi or fantasy food (which could include pies with live pigeons in them!), or preparing the recipes they find in the research portion.

"Filk" Songs:
Science Fiction Folk Songs

This program is inspired by a scene in the documentary *Trekkies* where filk singers are passionate and hilarious at the same time. While it is a lesser-exposed corner of fandom, it is a way to involve music, singing, or song-writing for your teens. Even if they are not interested in writing or performing a song of their own, they will find the whole subculture and its activities silly and funny.

Goals: To learn about "filk songs," or science fiction folk songs, that have appeared in film or on TV, and to learn about how fans sing them in real life and at conventions, and for participants to practice writing a "filk song" of their own.

Primary Books and Media: Filk Hall of Fame website (http://filkontario. ca/filk-hall-of-fame/), especially the "Newbie" page (http://filkontario. ca/newbie-notes/); clips from *Trekkies*; clip from *Firefly* (TV show) episode "Jaynestown."

Learning Objectives: Participants will

- Transform a familiar rhyme or folk song into a filk song honoring their favorite science fiction or fantasy

Duration: 1 hour

Materials Needed:

- Tablet or computer with loud speakers
- Lyrics sheets to familiar folk songs such as "I Know an Old Woman Who Swallowed a Fly"

Instructions:

- Show the clips from the *Firefly* episode "Jaynestown," if available, or a YouTube video of the song "The Hero of Canton."

- Show clips from *Trekkies* of filk, or this YouTube video: https://www.youtube.com/watch?v=G4NzZ5wy2WM
- Instruct participants to identify filk songs connected to any fandom they are interested in. Guide them through searches to find video clips or lyrics of songs they might be interested in.
- Pass out lyric sheets for any folk songs that might be familiar to your participants, such as "Yankee Doodle," "I Know an Old Woman Who Swallowed a Fly," or others. Challenge participants to rewrite the lyrics featuring characters or situations from the SFF they like. For example, to the tune of "Yankee Doodle": "Batman was the dark knight, riding in the Batmo-bile. He caught the Joker in a trap and tricked him with a de-al."
- If desired, any musically inclined participants could be invited to bring their instruments. If you have a library guitar or ukulele, this is a good time to use it.

Pop-Up Con at the Library

Conventions—comic conventions, Star Trek conventions, feminist science fiction conventions like WisCon, or yearly rotating events like Worldcon—are where fans come together, meet creators, experience new releases and upcoming releases, and are able to buy books, toys, memorabilia, costumes or props, and so forth. There are often panels of directors, writers, and actors, as well as a dealers room where merchandise is sold. One way of implementing this at the library (without vendors or outside partners, for example) is to structure it around a costume/cosplay competition.

Goals: To learn about fan conventions, and for participants to act as a conference committee planning and executing a pop-up convention in the library. Have everyone bring in their memorabilia for show and tell; create things like postcards or magnets to sell/give away; include a monster makeup booth or special effects photo booth.

Primary Books and Media: Series books, such as *Buffy the Vampire Slayer, The Walking Dead,* and superhero graphic novels; clips from *Trekkies*; clips from *Galaxy Quest*; *The 5th Wave* by Rick Yancey; *Parasite* by Mira Grant (which takes place at a convention).

Additional Books and Media: Additional tie-in materials chosen by participants.

Learning Objectives: Participants will

- Learn the ingredients needed to stage and organize a convention
- Execute a mini convention in the library
- Research the next nearest local fan conventions

Duration: 2 hours of advance planning, 2 hours of pop-up convention

Materials Needed:

- Name tags
- Tables for setting up merchandise

Courtesy of Jere Keys, "New York Comic Con 2013: Booths in the exhibit hall at NYCC." https://www.flickr.com/photos/tyreseus/10216999656/in/album-72157636448982583/.

Instructions:

- Ask any participants if they have ever been to a science fiction, fantasy, gaming, horror, or other geek culture convention. If you have attended one, share your experience.
- Show clips from the conventions portrayed in *Trekkies* and *Galaxy Quest*. While *Trekkies* is ostensibly documentary and *Galaxy Quest* fiction, note the similarity with which convention stereotypes, especially about obsessive fans, play out. Remind them that both of these films are heightening the zany and intense parts of conventions and fan culture to be funny and entertaining.
- Brainstorm, on a white board, a list of things a good con should or could have, including:
  - Guests of honor (actors, writers, etc.)
  - Cosplay and/or a costume contest
  - Items on display or for sale such as action figures, models, T-shirts, and other memorabilia; at conventions, this is called the dealers room.
  - Autographing tables
  - Speakers, panels, talks, and so forth promoting particular fandoms, books, or movies/TV series
  - Food/concessions
  - Games, events, parties, celebrations
  - Awards ceremonies
- Using this list, divide the participants into "committees" made up of two or three people, and task them with organizing a plan for one of the categories above. One committee should be in charge in logistics, including location, date, time, and so forth. This could be the beginnings of an actual pop-up con at the library, or an exercise where participants are imagining and building the con of their dreams. Plug in the specifics for an actual con at your library as needed.

- For the pop-up con at the library, chose at least a day or two away, but not too far away from the program that coherence is lost. These pop-ups are meant to be executed quickly.
- In the last 60 minutes of the session, bring together the whole team and "bottom line" particular tasks to be completed in the last 30 minutes of the program, and in between now and the pop-up con, including:
  - Producing a flyer
  - Producing a program/schedule, including guest bios
  - Finding and arranging toys, action figures, books from the library collection, and so forth into a dealers table
  - Choosing award recipients and/or making certificates or statuettes (paper towel rolls and pipe cleaners, for example)
  - Dressing up in costume for the costume contest, or face painting/makeup contest, and so on
- Feel free to bridge gaps and pull all of these details together. Consider serving as a contest judge and/or recruiting other staff or community members to be guest of honor, but let this pop-up convention be intentionally messy. It is a learning experiment in practicing organizational and planning skills in a group.

Doctor Who Cubes

The Doctor from *Doctor Who* is a perennial favorite geek character, and, as played by Peter Capaldi in his most modern incarnation, remains a sharp, sarcastic, and arch hero whose adventures are witty, high-concept, silly, and unexpected all at the same time. This British franchise is also unique in that so many different actors have not only played this role, but have also defined their versions rather than all playing toward a standard Doctor. Soon there may be a new Doctor, perhaps finally a woman or a person of color. These cubes are a great technique for making a keepsake craft that can be adapted to many themes.

Goals: To learn about fan culture by making a paper cube featuring different actors who have played the iconic British character.

Primary Books and Media: Any Doctor Who comics or graphic novels; *Chicks Dig Time Lords: A Celebration of Doctor Who by the Women Who Love It*, edited by Lynne M. Thomas and Tara O'Shea; *Queers Dig Time Lords: A Celebration of Doctor Who by the LGBTQ Fans Who Love It*, edited by Sigrid Ellis and Michael Damian Thomas; clips from multiple *Doctor Who* series. If there is time for a full episode, a good choice is series 1, episode 13, "The Parting of the Ways," which shows the transformation of one Doctor (Christopher Eccleston) into the next (David Tennant).

Additional Books and Media: Access to this webpage provides an authoritative listing and images of the thirteen doctors to use as reference: http://www.doctorwho.tv/50-years/doctors/. If *Doctor Who* is not right for your community, consider other franchises where the same character has been played by different actors: Batman, Superman, and so forth.

Learning Objectives: Participants will

- Practice image research skills to find reference images
- Learn the history of the *Doctor Who* character
- Write a letter to their favorite Doctor

Duration: 2 hours

Materials Needed:

- Markers, crayons, or colored pencils
- Cube template (see http://www.timvandevall.com/templates/paper-cube-template/)
- Access to a computer and printer, if you and participants prefer to use photos printed from the Internet

Instructions:

- Cubes only have six sides, so direct participants to choose six of the available Doctors, or to use three cubes to include all incarnations.
- Prepare a list of the 13 actors who have played this character and their "Doctor number." Lead participants through image searches to find suitable images to print and collage onto their cubes. Demonstrate how they can refine image searches, by choosing image type, size options, file type, and so on. If desired, you can also limit (in Google image search) for images available for reuse with Creative Commons licenses.
- If you would rather have the participants draw miniature portraits of the Doctors, use the images found online as reference images.
- Draw or paste images onto all sides of the cube, and cut and tape up the cube template.
- Encourage participants to share and examine each other's cubes, and inspire them to create games with them, such as rolling them like dice to pit Doctor against Doctor, or rolling until they get the same Doctor facing up.

World Building 101

Imagine a place where it is never dark, or another place where there are no men left on Earth. Put yourself in the shoes of a young woman who has to fight in the Hunger Games, or in the wings of the flyers in Fran Wilde's *Updraft*. World building is what makes science fiction and fantasy possible: it is when the author sets the rules of the game and the laws of physics for their story. Completely flipped or just slightly twisted, these worlds are what draw fans so deeply into science fiction and fantasy, and also what make possible so many of the "extras" of fandom: invented languages, foods and cookbooks, theme parks, and so on.

Goals: To explore world building and settings in science fiction and fantasy, and to begin creating a rich original setting in an idea book.

Primary Books and Media: *Wonderbook* by Jeff VanderMeer; *About Writing: Seven Essays, Four Letters, & Five Interviews* by Samuel R. Delany; *The Inheritance Trilogy* by N. K. Jemisin; *Half Life* by Shelley Jackson; *City of Stairs* by Robert Jackson Bennett; *The Birthday of the World and Other Stories* by Ursula K. Le Guin; clips from James Cameron's *Avatar* (2009); *Glory O'Brien's History of the Future* by A. S. King.

In *Half Life*, contemporary America looks very different. There were atomic explosions that have contaminated the country, and a very large percentage of the population (say, comparable to LGBTQ Americans or another sizeable minority community) are conjoined twins in the configuration of two heads sharing one body, two arms, and two legs. The normality of this occurrence suffuses the setting of the novel with distinct differences that work on many levels to subtly and constantly remind readers they are in a different universe.

In the story "The Birthday of the World," Le Guin world builds on many levels. Most primary, the action in this novella takes place entirely on an ancient generational ship, which means that no one currently aboard it has ever lived or known any other place. It has been traveling through space for hundreds or thousands of years. There is an additional

Source: https://pixabay.com/en/miniature-sculpture-mini-world-toys-274548/.

layer of world building outside the ship, too, and this ship exists in a galaxy and has a distant planet as its destination.

The Inheritance Trilogy takes place in a world where gods walk among humans, and everyone lives on a massive tree, and *City of Stairs* depicts a fresh and inventive secondary world with different cultures, geographies, and political systems that bears few similarities to what we are familiar with.

Additional Books and Media: This comprehensive online guide by Patricia Wrede from the Science Fiction and Fantasy Writers Association (SFWA) is a handy reference: http://www.sfwa.org/2009/08/fantasy-worldbuilding-questions/; this blog post about common world-building errors may also be of use: http://io9.gizmodo.com/7-deadly-sins-of-worldbuilding-998817537, and this article by YA fantasy writer Malinda Lo: http://www.malindalo.com/2012/10/five-foundations-of-world-building/.

Learning Objectives: Participants will

- Practice core setting and world-building fictional strategies
- Draw, sketch, describe, and write a lookbook, which can be used for future creative projects
- Read and learn about excellent examples of world building

Duration: 3 hours, preferably over 3 or 4 days in a series

Materials Needed:

- Notebooks and/or sketchpads to serve as each participant's idea book
- Houseplants
- Clay
- Assorted craft supplies such as pipe cleaners, felt, glitter, and so forth
- Small stones

Instructions:

- Explain and define world building as the fictional and imaginary universe an author creates, which can be as large as billions of galaxies or as small as a room. World building means creating the setting in which the characters exist and the action takes place. It might be a world that resembles our own very closely, or not, and might deviate only in very specific ways (e.g., male bodies get pregnant instead of female ones, for example). It might be a world where magic is real and the only characters are sentient lobsters. The point to make is that this is where science fiction and fantasy creators are free to create their visions.
- Define secondary worlds as fictional universes in fantasy settings. Secondary worlds are versions of world building participants may be familiar with: Narnia, Oz, Middle Earth, and so forth.
- Explain that they are going to make an idea book, and pass out the notebooks for them to write, draw, or collage in.
- Read passages from the books above, prompting participants to pay attention to clues about setting, but also the kinds of setting details and information that let a reader know the author is referring to the rules of the world he or she has built. For example, "This room is red," versus "Every room in Walloonyia is red."
- Show clips from the beginning of the film *Avatar*.
- Consider different layers of world building, and prompt participants to decide if they will create a universe, a galaxy, a solar system, a planet, a country, an island, a town, and so forth. They may choose any level of elaboration.
- On the planet and solar system levels, have participants experiment with this planet orbits simulator (http://www.stefanom.org/spc/#/), which demonstrates what happens to orbits over time and why having three or four suns in the sky, while cool looking, might mean your solar system explodes in a hundred years. (Or maybe that's the world they meant to create!)

Source: https://pixabay.com/en/jupiter-callisto-jupiter-moon-moon-529959/.

- Continuing on the planet level, caution them against oversimplifying: a planet that is entirely ice-covered, or entirely underwater, or entirely populated by bloodsucking bats might look or sound cool, but physics and ecology indicate instead that planets likely to support life would also likely contain the same kind of geographical, climatic, and genetic diversity that Earth does.
- Prompt them to imagine what kinds of plants, animals, insects, and people (if any) their world might have. If they are thinking about smaller-scale worlds, these questions are still avenues to explore:
  - How is the food chain set up?
  - What languages do the peoples speak?
  - What levels of technology exist?
  - Are there levels of technology that are different from the ones on historical Earth?
  - Is the world governed by special rules (e.g., magic or thousands of years of nanotechnology, etc.)
  - What does the physical landscape look like?
- At this point, distribute the props and houseplants, and guide participants through a series of creation exercises in group note-taking format, where you offer a prompt, give everyone 3–5 minutes of silent writing, then everyone reads out their responses while the rest of the participants copy down notes. By the end of several rounds, participants have their own writing and notes and ideas from everyone else filling up their idea book.
  - For example, show a houseplant. Prompt every participant to write for 3 minutes about the kind of alien animal who would live on that houseplant.

- Then ask them to imagine that animal meeting another animal of its same species, and have them write the action of what happens in their encounter.
- Tell them to draw the animal that eats the animal they invented.
- Ask them to write about the very worst weather those animals have ever experienced.
- Continue iterating through prompts and questions about the rules of these worlds, and urge them to sketch and write as much as possible. If they are using versions of Earth, focus in on language and culture/customs questions, as well as:
  - What is the most significant historical event that has ever happened in this place?
  - Where do these people buy food? Where is their food grown? Who grows it?
  - Describe a wedding or funeral among these characters.
- Refer to the SFWA website article linked above for more criteria and questions.
- Let participants continue iterating their world and setting creations, incorporating images or other props.

Fairy Tales in Space!

This program asks participants to bend a familiar tale into a science fiction world. Using fairy tales makes it accessible to teens even if they aren't big readers, and you can leverage their knowledge and experience with these fairy and folk tales to stoke their creativity. This program plan prompts them to break down the essential elements of a fairy tale and to create a new world (in space, if desired) in which it can exist. Any and all twisting of the tale, the moral, the characters, and the setting will ensue!

Goals: To understand the role fairy tales and the hero's journey have in sci-fi and fantasy literature, and to read examples of modern versions in service of writing a brand-new retelling.

Primary Books and Media: *Scarlet* by Marissa Meyer; stories from *The Bloody Chamber* by Angela Carter, especially "The Bloody Chamber," "The Courtship of Mr. Lyon," and "The Werewolf."

Additional Books and Media: If there is time and space to extend this program over a longer time period (and read a longer text), use Malinda Lo's *Ash*, a young adult, queer retelling of Cinderella, as well as clips from *Into the Woods* (2014), directed by Rob Marshall.

In his essay "The Hero with a Thousand Faces," scholar Joseph Campbell describes the "hero's journey," a literary model of how a story is shaped, identified, and interpreted. The "journey" is a circular pattern of external and internal changes in a character as that character moves through a particular story. Everything from *The Odyssey* to *The Wizard of Oz* and *Harry Potter* can be described in terms of this pattern or model. Although the fairy tale characters we visit in the program activities below might not embody this model directly, encourage the participants to think about "archetypes," which you should define for them as characters who stand in for some real-life people, places, or things, and serve as excellent examples with unmistakable characteristics of those people, places, and things.

Source: https://pixabay.com/en/monster-fairy-tale-painting-fantasy-1118411/.

Learning Objectives: Participants will

- Learn about the literary criticism of fairy tales and the hero's journey as a story structure
- Close read a modern adaptation of a fairy tale
- Write a new retelling of a fairy or folktale

Duration: 2 hours; can be expanded into multiple sessions

Materials Needed:

- I recommend Google image searching a visual representation of the hero's journey, such as this one (http://saltlakecomiccon.com/wp-content/uploads/2014/09/herosjourney2.jpg), which also features an image of Mark Hamill as Luke Skywalker.

Instructions:

- Read one of the Angela Carter stories aloud. Pair it with a picture book version of the more familiar tale.
- Moderate a discussion that focuses on how Carter "bent" the tale:
  - What core elements from the familiar fairy tale are still there?
  - What did she change subtly?
  - What did she change that is more substantial?
  - What did she add?

- Show clips from *Into the Woods* and ask a similar set of questions. Make a list, as a group, of what the reinventors kept and what they changed.
- From the picture books available, ask each participant to select a story.
- Direct them to read the story, and decide on a core list of four to five elements they will keep in their space adaptation.
- Prompt them to transform the setting: Where else could this tale take place and still have an effect on readers? If they take the title of the program literally and set it in space, which is a good challenge, remind them that physical laws we are used to work differently in space and that they will have to think through these fundamental shifts as they retell the story.
- Pause and let participants discuss in pairs or small groups what they will be changing about the story. Ask them to serve as a first reviewer for their peers, and a check on whether or not the author's adaptation direction makes sense and will help tell a new version of the folktale.
- Let students write and revise in pairs for up to an hour. In the last half hour of the program, invite them to tell their story. They can use notes and read verbatim, if they must, but remind them that folktales were originally part of our oral culture and were meant to be told aloud. In addition, they can use sketches or pictures to help them retell their story, kamishibai-style, if desired.

Sonnets from Saturn: Science Fiction Poetry

Consider this program during a creative writing series that pulls in other imaginative writing experiences from these plans, or during National Poetry Month in April. The short texts make this workshop very accessible, and you can always substitute in excellent children's poetry at your discretion. Adam Rex and Shel Silverstein are good places to start.

Goals: To learn about the world of science fiction poetry, and practice writing a poem (a sonnet or haiku) with science fiction elements.

Primary Books and Media: "About Science Fiction Poetry" by Suzette Haden Elgin (http://www.sfwa.org/members/elgin/SFPoetry.html) and Paul Cook's counterpoint "Why Science Fiction Poetry Is Embarrassingly Bad" (http://amazingstoriesmag.com/2013/02/why-science-fiction -poetry-is-embarrassingly-bad/).

Additional Books and Media: Science Fiction Poetry Association website (http://sfpoetry.com/).

The sonnet is a form that, at its most basic, allows a writer to juxtapose two contrasting ideas or images. Print out the rhyme scheme pattern and examples found here: http://www.sonnets.org/basicforms.htm.

A haiku is another basic poetry form that relies on essentializing language—that is, boiling it down and presenting the most essential characteristics of the idea or image. Print out the syllable pattern and examples found here: https://www.poets.org/poetsorg/text/haiku-poetic-form.

Younger participants may find it easier to use haiku because of its length and simplicity. Chose which form will work the best with your group, or, with advanced participants, challenge them to tackle the same science fiction idea or image in both poetic forms.

Learning Objectives: Participants will

- Close read poems
- Practice a poetic form (haiku or sonnet) and draft a poem; younger participants could create an acrostic poem or a book spine poem, if desired

Duration: 1 hour

Materials Needed:

- Paper for journaling
- Sample poems
- 15–20 books from the YA science fiction section of the library

Instructions:

- Read and discuss the examples from sfpoetry.com.
- Explain the structure of the poetic form you will ask them to create, and offer at least one sample of that poem (available at the links above).
- Close read the sample poem, and discuss it terms of both form and content, pointing out how it uses language and imagery to elaborate an idea or tell of an action.
- Distribute the 15–20 science fiction books, and tell participants to use these books: their cover illustrations, the titles themselves, as well as any details about plot, character, or author they can glean from the jackets will serve as their poetic inspiration.
- Let participants write and experiment with their forms and these books as inspiration. Circulate among the group to offer feedback and encouragement.
- Bring the entire group together, and ask for volunteers to share their poems.
- If desired, participants could also make SFF book spine poetry from these sample books.
- The group may also wish to compile everyone's poems into a chapbook to print and make available in the library.

Dinos versus Dragons: Ultimate Smackdown

Dinosaurs appear in a lot of science fiction (and some fantasy) and capture imaginations from a young age. Dragons are nearly as present, although mostly in fantasy, and are the only mythical beast that can size up against the very real but very extinct dinosaur. This program prompts participants to think creatively and critically while they compare and contrast these fearsome creatures.

Goals: To engage the tropes of science fiction and fantasy to stage a debate about whether dinosaurs or dragons would win in a final showdown.

Primary Books and Media: "A Sound of Thunder" in *Dinosaur Tales* by Ray Bradbury; "Triceratops Summer" in *The Dog Said Bow-Wow* by Michael Swanwick; *Jurassic Park* by Michael Crichton;. *Eragon* by Christopher Paolini; *A Natural History of Dragons: A Memoir by Lady Trent* by Marie Brennan; clips from any Jurassic Park movie; clips from *Game of Thrones* TV series; clips from *Eragon* (2006), directed by Stefen Fangmeier.

Learning Objectives: Participants will

- Research the literary history of dragons
- Research the role of dinosaurs in classics of science fiction
- Construct and provide evidence for arguments in favor of either dragons or dinosaurs

Duration: 1–2 hours of research and to prepare arguments; 1 hour of debate. Can stage the debate as a public event.

Materials Needed:

- Whiteboard or butcher paper
- Computers or tablets for guided Internet searches

Source: https://pixabay.com/en/dino-dinosaur-tyrannosaurus-rex-648717/.

Instructions:

- Explain to the group that the goal of this program is to stage a debate about dragons and dinosaurs. The point is not necessarily to pick one creature over the other, but rather to build arguments about the ways in which they are similar and how they are different.
- Read short passages aloud from the books above, at least three passages each for dinosaurs and three for dragons. Remind them that although dinosaurs actually existed, they are reading science-fiction versions of dinosaurs.
- Show clips from the recommended movies. This will be especially useful in terms of describing the differences in appearance, movement, and behavior of these two sets of "animals."
- As a large group, start a group Venn diagram comparing and contrasting dinosaurs and dragons.
- Ask a series a questions, which will end up being the terms of the debate:
  - What did they eat?
  - How did they/do they interact with people?
  - Do they interact with other actual or fantasy creatures?
  - Do they have special powers or abilities (like flight)?
  - How do they look? How are their bodies similar or different?

- How do they move? What do their arms, legs, wings, bodies, necks, and so on look like in locomotion?
  - How big were/are they?
  - How long is their life span?
  - Where in the world are they found?
  - Which being is more dangerous? To whom and in what context?
- After 15 minutes or so of discussion, divide the group into two expert teams, Team Dinosaur and Team Dragon. Direct them, in their teams, to research and construct 5–10 arguments about the superiority of their subject. "Superiority" in this sense can be literal markers—they are faster, they are stronger, they can travel greater distances—or more abstract ideas, such as dinosaurs are "superior" because they actually existed and we know more about them because there is a fossil record. Circulate between the two groups to give feedback.
- Stage the debate. Flip a coin to see who goes first. Teams should present their brief argument, then the supporting evidence. The opposing team can then rebut their arguments and present ideas and supporting evidence of their own to make a counterpoint. Proceed in a point-counterpoint manner until all the arguments have been presented.
- Ask all participants to vote on which "animal" is "better" and would win an ultimate smackdown, or appoint yourself arbiter and decide which team presented more convincing arguments and evidence.

Fifty-Five-Minute Fanzine

Library teens will flock to this program in which they can write and produce their own zine, which will be available in the library. It makes them into content makers and contributors to the critical conversations in fandom. Depending on your access to computers and software, consider making available a two- or four-page print template to plug pictures and articles into. If your teens are interested, continue making additional issues of the magazine.

Goals: To learn about fanzines, or fan-produced magazines, their role in science fiction and fantasy fandom, and to make one in the span of an hour.

Primary Books and Media: *Fanzines: The DIY Revolution* by Teal Triggs.

Additional Books and Media: Covers of other fanzines for inspiration available here: http://fanzines.tumblr.com/.

Fanzines are magazines, but they sprang up in an era when fans could not contact each other and share their enthusiasm for science fiction and fantasy online, whether via message board or Snapchat. Fanzines grew out of conventions, which were the place for fans to connect and think/talk/write/argue about their favorite books, shows, and movies, and the fan newsletter became a way for them to continue those discussions even while they were not all together at a convention.

Learning Objectives: Participants will

- Practice writing different kinds of articles
- Understand the role of fanzines in SFF fan culture

Duration: 1.5 hours, with 55 minutes devoted to producing the fanzine

Materials Needed:

- Computers/printing for typing, if desired
- Photocopier access to make copies of the zine

Instructions:

- Explain to participants what fanzines are, and that today they are being assembled into an expert team of journalists and editors who will work together to produce one in the next 55 minutes.
- Show examples of fanzines, the covers and interiors. Let the group know that there are no strict limits on content, and that anything having to do with science fiction or fantasy literature, media, video games, board games, and so forth can have a place. This should only take 10 minutes or so. Remember, you are all on deadline!
- Suggest that they build their fanzine from the following ingredients of fanzines:
  - One feature article—a longer, in-depth article about something or someone that might use interview or review as part of its sources, but also synthesizes other sources to make a more substantial point or tell a deeper story, say about the making of a film
  - One actor interview—participants should identify an actor or actress to create a fake interview with. Because they will be making it up, the person could be an invented person, or an actor who is well known in the genre such as Patrick Stewart, Kristen Stewart, Jennifer Lawrence, or so forth
  - One writer interview—they should select an author (living or dead) to fake interview, as well. Consider tying these choices together with a theme (i.e., if you are interviewing someone from the cast of a movie about robots, perhaps the author is Isaac Asimov)
  - One book review—a short summary and opinion of an SFF book
  - One movie/TV review—the same but for media
  - Illustrations—whether drawings or photos and collages, the best zines will have pictures, too
- Run the editorial meeting by writing up this list of ingredients and asking people for story pitches or ideas for these categories. Make assignments based on who volunteers. Anyone without pitch ideas could become the managing editor, who will be responsible for putting all of the articles together in one document.
- Set a timer for 55 minutes. Tell everyone the managing editor needs their drafts in 50 minutes or less. In the meantime, the managing editor should start working on a cover, and you should circulate, offering help with searches, writing, coming up with details, refining interview questions, improving illustrations, and so forth.
- Assist the managing editor in gathering all the articles physically or electronically, and then make a copy of the whole zine to distribute to the participants.

Ewe? Ew: Rules for Cloning and Genetic Engineering

Cloning is a great jumping-off point for including STEM area content, as well as engaging young people in discussions about scientific ethics and the application of technology to biological life. In particular, this could be a great place to talk about genetically modified organisms (GMOs) and their role in our food system, and help them build media literacy, too. There are a great many clones in science fiction and fantasy literatures, and you and your teens should have no trouble connecting to the texts I suggest or finding others that suit your community.

Goals: To learn about real-life genetic science in cloning and genetic engineering, and to explore the ethical implications of cloning in sci-fi.

Additional Books and Media: *Never Let Me Go* by Kazuo Ishiguro; any stories from *Daily Science Fiction*'s (an online magazine) free archive of cloning stories (http://dailysciencefiction.com/science-fiction/clones), especially "Seeking Nothing" by Cat Rambo, "The Ambiguity Clock" by Lavie Tidhar, or "Still Life" by A. C. Wise, all of which are available at that link; clips from *Gattaca* (1997) directed by Andrew Niccol; clips from *The Island* (2005), directed by Michael Bay; clips from *Alien: Resurrection* (1997), directed by Jean-Pierre Jeunet, for graphic sequences involving the failed clones of Sigourney Weaver's character, Ellen Ripley; clips from *Jurassic Park* (1993), directed by Steven Spielberg, especially the sequence explaining how they cloned dinosaurs, which is available here: https://www.youtube.com/watch?v=iMsJe3TymqY.

The name of this program is inspired by Dolly, a famous cloned sheep from the 1990s, who was one of the first successfully cloned animals. Read more about her here: http://www.nms.ac.uk/explore/stories/natural-world/dolly-the-sheep/. The "ew" part of the name refers to the ethical implications of cloning and genetic engineering, namely that individual animals and people can be harmed and can experience pain in cloning processes, and that it lets people tinker with the abilities and characteristics of others. A common complaint about cloning and genetic engineering is that it lets scientists create things that would not necessarily be found in nature.

Learning Objectives: Participants will

- Explore the ethical implications of cloning and genetic engineering of humans
- Draft and construct their personal set of rules for cloning

Duration: 2 hours

Materials Needed:

- Whiteboard or butcher paper with markers

Instructions:

- Describe the plot of the movie *The Island,* and show clips from the end.
- Show the "Mr. DNA" sequence from *Jurassic Park* linked above.
- Direct users to find an online article about cloning and genetic modification. Give them 15–20 minutes of active searching and reading, and let them know they need to bring back the following facts from their articles to the larger group:
  - What is the most surprising thing they learned in this research?
  - What is the most beneficial thing cloning could do?
  - What is the most harmful or dangerous thing according to the article they read?
- Bring participants back together to report these facts.
- Read one of the sample short stories aloud. They are all under 2,000 words, and can easily be shared in their entirety.
- Moderate a discussion that bridges their nonfiction reading and the facts they reported with the cloning or genetic modification happening in the story.
- As a group, on a whiteboard or butcher paper, make a long list of concerns about cloning.
- Refine the list of concerns, and challenge participants to condense them into a series of rules. Share and discuss the rules they create. Consider posting them in the library.

Interview with an Android

The title of this program is inspired by the classic vampire novel *Interview with a Vampire*, by Anne Rice, but focuses on the technological end of these SFF literatures, with teens digging into famous robots, androids, and cyborgs. Consider linking this program up with other creative writing exercises, stressing that the form of an interview is great technical writing practice where writers can especially craft voice, point of view, and narration.

Goals: To explore the role artificial and mechanical life plays in sci-fi and fantasy to prepare a radio interview of a famous android, cyborg, or other robot.

Primary Books and Media: *Boilerplate* by Paul Guinan and Anina Bennett; *The Alchemy of Stone* by Ekaterina Sedia; clips of Data from *Star Trek: The Next Generation* (TV show); clips of Cylons from *Battlestar Galactica* (2004 TV show); clips of WALL-E and EVE from Disney's *WALL-E*; clips of Bender from *Futurama* (TV show).

Additional Books and Media: Picture books for younger participants: *Robot Dog* by Mark Oliver; *Boy + Bot* by Ame Dyckman; *Oh No!: Or How My Science Project Destroyed the World* by Mac Barnett.

Learning Objectives: Participants will

- Research fictional robots and androids
- Practice writing conversational interview questions
- Exercise creative writing by constructing interview answers
- Present their interview to the group

Duration: 2.5 hours

Materials Needed:

- Notepads

Source: https://pixabay.com/en/android-robot-technology-cyborg-770062/.

Instructions:

- Instruct participants that they will be playing two roles in this pro-gram, reporter and subject. They will need to flex creative writing muscle (perhaps in pairs) to create both the questions and answers to an interview with an android.
- Show the book *Boilerplate*. Explain that it is a (convincing) hoax, and that there was no such robot. Point out how easy it is to believe that Boilerplate existed!
- Briefly discuss differences between artificial life-forms, including robots, androids, cyborgs, automatons, artificial intelligence, bio-bots, and so forth. Use Wikipedia or dictionary definitions, or dig into a slice of fandom represented by message boards like this one: http://scifi.stackexchange.com/questions/11000/whats-the-difference-between-cyborgs-and-androids.
- Show clips of androids, cyborgs, robots, and so on from the movies and TV shows above. Ask participants which of these characters they might already be familiar with.
- As a group, brainstorm some things that are common to all of these forms of artificial life, and also what things differ between them.
- Assign partners, and ask each pair to use a fictional character android, cyborg, robot, or so forth to interview.
- As a group, brainstorm general interview questions, which may include:
  - Who created you?
  - Do you eat?
  - How long will you live?

- What is your power source?
- What are your special capabilities?
- Are you dangerous to people? Helpful to people?
- Do you live with people? Have you always lived with people?
- What does a particular food taste or smell like to you?
- What makes you sad? What makes you happy?

- Ask the pairs to spend 30–40 minutes finalizing their questions, and then making up answers in the voice or guise of their robot subject. If necessary, they can do additional research online to help them come up with believable answers. Tell them they are aiming to finalize around five meaty questions and answers (i.e., open-ended questions that cannot just be answered with a yes/no) to present to the group.
- Bring them back together. Groups should show a picture of their android interview subject, and then portray reporter and robot asking and answering questions. Some pairs might be up for additional, unscripted questions from the rest of the group, if desired.

Part Three

READING AND CREATIVE WRITING PROGRAMS

Creative Writing Exercises

The following exercises are meant to expose participants to writing experiments, prompts, and strategies that excite them about reading, writing, or producing science fiction and fantasy work. Emphasize continually that all writing in these workshops should be considered disposable experiments and drafts upon which your young writers can keep building. The intent is not to put these participants through a traditional workshop, or for them to workshop the fruits of these exercises in groups.

For detailed studies in the craft of fiction, especially science fiction, see *About Writing* by Samuel R. Delany, *Wonderbook* by Jeff VanderMeer, *Storyteller: Writing Lessons and More from 27 Years of the Clarion Writers' Workshop* by Kate Wilhelm, or one of many other titles. For the purposes of these workshops, there is one overarching rule and goal to impart: writers should write as clearly and concisely as possible. Write what you mean, and read it back to see if it makes any sense. Know the definitions of the words you use, even if they "sound good." Don't use three or four words when one or two will do. Encouraging participants to improve on the sentence level will help ground them in writing fiction (as well as in reading and writing for school!), even in these very short workshops.

For motivated writers, turn them toward other print and Web resources about the craft of writing. Encourage them to explore this guide to overused tropes (http://tvtropes.org/pmwiki/pmwiki.php/Main/TheGrandListOfOverusedScienceFictionCliches), which can help them self-edit and improve their writing. There is also a science fiction writing camp for teens every year called Shared Worlds (https://www.wofford.edu/sharedworlds/default.aspx) and communities on the online writing community Wattpad.

Write a Space Opera in an Hour

Space opera is one of the quintessential flavors of science fiction, with characteristics recognizable even to non-fans. While you can think of it like a soap opera in space (see *Dark Matter*, any incarnation of Star Trek, or *Firefly*), recent interpretations have brought fresh, new space worlds to reader attention. Ann Leckie's *Ancillary Justice* combines humans and ships in an original way, and James S. A. Corey's *The Expanse* series eschews clichés like faster-than-light travel and keeps its space fleets in our vast solar system. Space opera can include many kinds of military or anthropological science fiction, and much more.

Goals: To understand the ingredients of a space opera, a mode of often-hard science fiction writing about space travel, interstellar empires, epic battles, and vast expanses of space and time.

Primary Books and Media: *Ancillary Justice* by Ann Leckie; *Shards of Honor* by Lois McMaster Bujold; "The Birthday of the World" in *The Birthday of the World and Other Stories* by Ursula K. Le Guin; clips from *Battlestar Galactica* (2004); clips from *Star Wars* (1977); *All You Need Is Kill* by Ryosuke Takeuchi.

Additional Books and Media: *The Mammoth Book of SF Wars* edited by Ian Watson and Ian Whates. London: Robinson, 2012.

Learning Objectives: Participants will

- Learn about the form of the space opera
- Engage fictional strategies of planning setting, plot, and character in a controlled writing experiment
- Practice imaginative writing in a sustained burst

Duration: 2 hours

Materials Needed:

- Consider using this science fiction, fantasy, and role-playing name generator for inspiration: http://www.springhole.net/writing _roleplaying_randomators/sf_namegens.htm.

Source: https://pixabay.com/en/science-fiction-soldier-spaceship-965259/.

Instructions:

- In the first 30 minutes, share the story and video clips. Ask participants to take notes while they watch, paying particular attention to anything they determine is an "ingredient" of space opera.
- Together, in a large group, list the elements or "ingredients" that they noticed.
- For the next 15 minutes, focus in on a smaller set of elements, being sure to include:
    - Ship. This signifies setting: time frame, level of technology, and so on.
    - Crew. Describe the characters: who they are, what they want, where they are going.
    - Route. Again, this relates to the setting: Are they in the core of the galactic empire or running a mail route to outer settlements? Is there a galactic empire, a federation of worlds, a home world and a distant colony? Are there aliens? Route should also lead to plot: Where are they going and how long is it taking? What are they doing along the way?
    - Problem. What is the conflict: What stands in between what the characters want and where they are going? Conflict should be organized into smaller units of conflict expressed in action (i.e., in plot).

- Map these four and their corresponding fictional elements (setting, conflict, character, and plot) and discuss specific passages from the texts at hand that demonstrate them well. For Leckie's book, there is a lot to say about character and setting, for example. In the Bujold book, plot events elegantly build and sustain conflict and give time for rich characterizations, especially of Cordelia, to emerge.
- Individually or in pairs, have participants spend time brainstorming ideas for their own space opera based on elaborating these four elements: ship, crew, route, and problem.
- Direct them to write for an hour. Remind them that their stories can be as short as a long paragraph: the goal here should not be length, but rather the creation of a fictional world where the readers clearly understand who/what the ship, crew, route, and problem are.
- In the last 15 minutes of the program, invite participants to share their stories, at least in part.

Write a Sword and Sorcery Story in an Hour

Sword and sorcery is fantasy writing that, traditionally, draws inspiration from medieval Europe and features magic rather than advanced technology. Current writers are perfecting and reinventing this genre by taking inspiration from beyond Europe. Kai Ashante Wilson's *The Sorcerer of the Wildeeps* is a perfect cutting-edge example of this genre.

Goals: To study and explore the characteristics of a primary mode of fantasy writing, sword and sorcery, and to plan and outline the story in one hour.

Primary Books and Media: *Graceling* by Kristin Cashore; *The Sorcerer of the Wildeeps* by Kai Ashante Wilson; *A Knight of the Seven Kingdoms* (graphic novel) by George R. R. Martin; *Swordspoint* by Ellen Kushner; *Sword of the Rightful King: A Novel of King Arthur* by Jane Yolen.

Additional Books and Media: *The Mists of Avalon* by Marion Zimmer Bradley.

Learning Objectives: Participants will

- Close read example passages and unpack the fantasy elements
- Outline and sketch out a sword and sorcery fantasy story

Duration: 2 hours

Instructions:

- In the first 30 minutes, share the story. Ask participants to take notes while they read, discussing the elements of setting, character, conflict, and plot.
- Together, in a large group, list the elements or "ingredients" they noticed.
- For the next 15 minutes, focus in on a smaller set of elements as they relate to setting, conflict, character, and plot. Brainstorm with these questions:

Source: https://pixabay.com/en/lego-children-toys-colorful-play-674340/.

- Who (character)
- What (plot/conflict)
- When/where (setting)
- Why (conflict)
- Map these four and their corresponding fictional elements (setting, conflict, character, and plot) and discuss specific passages from the texts at hand that demonstrate them well. Individually or in pairs, participants should spend time brainstorming ideas for their own sword and sorcery story based on elaborating these four central questions of who, what, when/where, and why.
- Direct them to write for an hour. Remind them that their stories need only be several sentences that build on each other. They should aim to create a fictional world where the readers clearly understand the social setup of the land they have created, in terms of social class or of occupation (like farming), where the main action of the story is taking place, and what the rules of the road are: Is there magic? How does it work? Are there fictional beings or creatures like dragons or elves? This is their time to think big. In the last 15 minutes of the program, invite participants to share their stories, at least in part.

Write a Dystopia/Utopia in an Hour

Dystopias are probably one of the most popular genres of SF at the moment, especially in books, movies, and TV, so overexposed that some fans might have had enough. Utopias are less common, and usually, in our popular entertainments, are too-good-to-be-true masks hiding terrifying dystopias in the cellar. These kinds of stories make us face our heaviest fears by making them a normal part of a world, and are disturbing distractions to our own changing climate, natural disasters, migrant crises, and devastating wars.

Goals: To explore dystopias and utopias and how science fiction writers use dystopias and utopias to write about humanity's real-life problems, and to create a dystopian or utopian world.

Primary Books and Media: *The Giver* by Lois Lowry; *Glory O'Brien's History of the Future* by A. S. King; "When It Changed" by Joanna Russ (http://boblyman.net/englt392/texts/When%20It%20Changed.pdf); *The Handmaid's Tale* by Margaret Atwood; *The Hunger Games* by Suzanne Collins; *Feed* by M. T. Anderson; clips from the History Channel's "Life after People" (from YouTube or http://www.history.com/shows/life-after-people).

Learning Objectives: Participants will

- Dissect a classic dystopia or utopia and conjecture about its relationship to real life
- Create a dystopian or utopian setting and sketch out a story that could take place in it

Source: https://pixabay.com/en/graffiti-man-fantasy-dream-1224886/.

Duration: 2 hours

Instructions:

- In the first 30 minutes, share the story and video clips. Ask participants to take notes while they read, discussing the elements of setting, character, conflict, and plot.
- Together, in a large group, list the elements or "ingredients" they noticed.
- For the next 15 minutes, focus in on a smaller set of elements as they relate to setting, conflict, character, and plot. Brainstorm with these questions:

- Who (character)
- What (plot/conflict)
- When/where (setting)
- Why (conflict)
- Spend considerable time on the when/where question. What makes this world (this utopia or dystopia) different from our world? How is it similar? Is it more similar than different?
- Map these four and their corresponding fictional elements (setting, conflict, character, and plot) and discuss specific passages from the texts at hand that demonstrate them well. Individually or in pairs, participants should spend time brainstorming ideas for their own dystopia or utopia based on elaborating these four central questions of who, what, when/where, and why.
- Direct them to write for an hour. Inspire them to consider the fundamental questions of a dystopia: Where and when are we? What kind of disaster(s) happened to get us here? Who survived? How? How do the characters find or keep shelter, food, and so forth?
- In the last 15 minutes of the program, invite participants to share their stories, at least in part.

Write a First Contact Story in an Hour

This workshop is harder than it seems, because participants have to invent an alien and fit it into a plot meeting humans for the first time. You could encourage participants to consider the encounter from the point of view of the alien. Challenge advanced writers to consider this workshop from the point of view of an animal familiar to us—whales, jellyfish, cows—encountering a human.

Goals: This program will expose participants to a first contact story, in which a writer captures the very first encounter(s) between aliens and people, and encourage them to write their own.

Primary Books and Media: "Amnesty" in *Bloodchild and Other Stories* by Octavia E. Butler; *Dawn* by Octavia E. Butler; "Cold-Blooded" in *Good Bones and Simple Murders* by Margaret Atwood; *The 5th Wave* by Rick Yancey.

Additional Books and Media: *A Paradigm of Earth* by Candas Jane Dorsey; *A Darkling Sea* by James Cambias.

Learning Objectives: Participants will

- Close read a first contact story and analyze both the construction of the aliens and the dramatic moments of "first contact"
- Draw/sketch a concept for an alien species
- Dramatize the action of the first time that alien species encounters humans

Duration: 2 hours

Instructions:

- In the first 30 minutes, share the story "Amnesty." Ask participants to take notes while they read, discussing the elements of setting, character, conflict, and plot. Focus on the aliens and how Butler makes them convincing. Additionally, they seem very different from humans on the visual or genetic level; are they very different emotionally? Or in terms of their relationship to power?

- Together, in a large group, list the elements or "ingredients" they noticed. Brainstorm with these questions:
  - Who (character)
  - What (plot/conflict)
  - When/where (setting)
  - Why (conflict)
- Map these four and their corresponding fictional elements (setting, conflict, character, and plot) and discuss specific passages from the texts at hand that demonstrate them well. Individually or in pairs, participants should then spend time brainstorming ideas for their own first contact story based on elaborating these four central questions of who, what, when/where, and why.
- Ask them to focus on the human and alien "who" of this story, although it is possible that the alien is revealed as a what or when/where, depending on the particular idea. Ask them to list 10 adjectives that describe the alien they are creating, and to make a 10-minute sketch of it.
- Direct the group to write for an hour. Participants should not worry about length, but rather focus on the beginnings of their story that will situate the reader into when and where they are, what kind of spaceships are involved (if any), what the alien looks/feels/smells/thinks like, and so forth.
- In the last 15 minutes of the program, invite participants to share their stories, at least in part.

Write Alternate History in an Hour

This workshop prompts participants to ask the ultimate what-if question, the answer to which radically changes our present and future. Consider doing this program in conjunction with a social studies or history teacher partner, who might be able to help you match up your final book selection to what your teens are studying in class. While this is not necessary for a robust program, it is useful if students have familiarity with the history they are slanting into a new fictional world.

Goals: To explore another SF subgenre, alternate history, demonstrating to participants how authors recast the past in the service of storytelling, and encourage them to create their own alternate timelines.

Primary Books and Media: *The Freedom Maze* by Delia Sherman; *Wolf by Wolf* by Ryan Graudin; *Zulu Heart* by Steven Barnes; *Among Others* by Jo Walton; clips from *Sliding Doors* (1998), directed by Peter Howitt.

Additional Books and Media: *Dreadnought* by Cherie Priest; *Abraham Lincoln: Vampire Hunter* by Seth Grahame-Smith.

Learning Objectives: Participants will

- Practice the forms of alternate history
- Research real historical events and create a "twist" for them
- Write a fictional timeline of alternate events

Duration: 2 hours

Materials Needed:

- Writing materials
- Computer for showing the movie clip

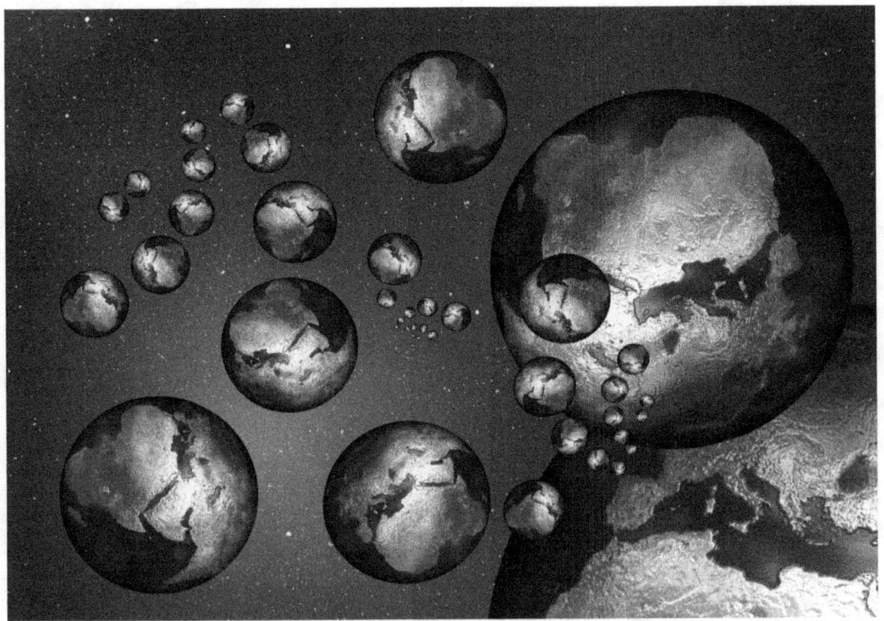

Source: https://pixabay.com/en/globe-earth-country-continents-73397/.

Instructions:

- In the first 30 minutes, share the story and video clips. Ask participants to take notes while they read, discussing the elements of setting, character, conflict, and plot.
- For the next 15 minutes, focus on the when/where question of setting. The purpose of alternate history is to majorly "twist" our expectations around time frame. Ask participants: What is different about the history in this world? What are the consequences for the characters in the story?
- Map these four questions—who, what, when/where, why—and their corresponding fictional elements (setting, conflict, character, and plot) and discuss specific passages from the texts at hand that demonstrate them well. Individually or in pairs, participants can then spend time brainstorming ideas for their own alternate history based on elaborating these four central questions of who, what, when/where, and why.
- Direct them to write for an hour. Remind them that their stories can be as short as a long paragraph: the goal here should not be length, but rather the creation of a fictional world where the readers can put themselves in the when and why of the twisted history and understand how historical or current events are different in

this version, and what the key departures from "normal" history consist of.

- In the last 15 minutes of the program, invite participants to share their stories, at least in part.

Spellcraft

Everyone can pretend to be a witch with this program, which is a fun way to inspire your participants' creativity. They will make up spells based on what is important to (or bothering) them, and it can be a great opportunity for you to get to know what is on their minds. It can also be a robust writing exercise, and some teens might consider their spells as short poems.

Goals: To highlight an important ingredient in fantasy writing, magic spells and spellcraft, and to encourage participants to write their own spells.

Primary Books and Media: *Carry On* by Rainbow Rowell; *Harry Potter*, or Lev Grossman's *The Magicians* for more mature audiences; clips of spellcraft from the many Harry Potter films. Google video searches of "Harry Potter spells" lead to many videos, including this supercut from several of the movies in the series: https://www.youtube.com/watch?v=cV2E41Q6OvY.

Additional Books and Media: This Harry Potter fan wiki has a compendium of spells that may be interesting as additional examples: http://harrypotter.wikia.com/wiki/Spell_creation.

Learning Objectives: Participants will

- Consider the way spells and spellcraft further a fantasy or magical setting
- Practice making up names for imaginary spells
- Create several imaginary spells based on the examples or models provided

Duration: 1 hour or less

Materials Needed: (These are a sampling; other objects can be substituted.)

- A wand
- An iron nail
- A telescope

Source: https://pixabay.com/en/witch-magic-bounce-magic-wand-1112643/.

- Strands of hair from you or someone else
- Leaves, flowers, and needles from trees
- Coins, especially old ones or ones from other countries
- Rocks or stones
- Household items like salt and water

Instructions:

- Start this program with a disclaimer that magic is not real and that you will be playing a game of pretend and these spells are just for fun. The language of the program engages on a level where it could be real, and participants will have more fun that way, but it is necessary not to confuse younger children or worry parents.
- Read and share examples of the spellcraft of Harry Potter, both from the books and from the movies. Ask participants what their favorite spells from this series are, and what other spells they would want to create.
- Tell them that you are going to share some additional spells and teach them the tricks to making up their own.
- Tell them that magic is old and unreliable. These spells are very old and come from many different places around the world. Because they have been translated from other languages and passed down for years before coming to you, young magician, you must rely on your own magical knowledge and instinct to make them work.

Be careful! Magical energies are all around every object, and usually are in balance. When magicians tinker with magical energies, sometimes the energies become unbalanced.

- Give them rules: Do not try to hurt anyone else with your magic. If you do, your magic will hurt you first.
- Instruct participants that most spells need just an incantation. Sometimes they need an object or objects to help the magician direct the magical energy. Some of the most common magical items include those listed in the "Materials Needed" section above.
- Let them know that some of these objects you may already have, and some you have to gather. Magicians can always make substitutions. If you cannot find a bronze coin from ancient Rome, for example, a regular penny might work.
- Share with them three sample spells:

Cool Down

Best for summer days without shade or for times when you want to calm down after a magical battle or very tiring spell.

- Close your eyes and plug your ears with your fingers.
- Say the following incantation:

An icy trickle down my back, a cool breeze will make me sneeze,
Take away this heat with ease.
An icy trickle on my neck, a frosty glass of water: this heat my spell will slaughter!

Frustration

This spell works two ways, so you have to be careful. The first way it works is that you can frustrate someone or something. But the second way will send that frustration back at your own efforts! So be careful! In magic, any negative energy needs positive energy to balance it out. So if you try and frustrate someone else, the magical energy might end up frustrating you.

You will need: a pinch of dust from the corner of your room, a strand of hair from an adult, and a nail.

- Wrap the strand of hair around the nail and sprinkle the dust on it.
- While you are concentrating on whatever you want to frustrate, say the following incantation:

Frustes mustes doo. Frustes mustes foo.
Repeat over and over again for 10 seconds.

Night Vision

If the power goes out, or you wake up in the middle of the night, you might use this spell. (It sometimes works better if you repeat the incantation backward.)

- Open your eyes as wide as they will go, and take two deep breaths.
- Point to your eyes with the thumb of your left hand.
- Say this incantation very slowly:

> One spark will fill the dark,
> but one spark I don't need.
> Ghostlight, moonlight, dragonlight or even all three: glow as long as I need to see.

- Now, using these samples as models, direct each participant to spend 20 minutes making up a spell and creating the incantation or action that could trigger it.
- To conclude the program, bring them back into a big group and have them demonstrate and teach their spells to the whole group.

From Elvish to Klingon: Science-Fiction and Fantasy Languages to Know

Science-fiction and fantasy languages are an important tool writers and directors use to really convince their readers and watchers of authenticity. Whether speaking a completely fictional language or using an ancient or extinct human language, fluent characters help sell the world someone has built. In many cases, qualified linguists have created these fictional languages and made them scientifically sound. This could also be a jumping-off point for interested participants to read about other constructed languages, such as Esperanto.

Goals: To learn about constructed languages (conlangs) and the communities that use them, and to explore what it takes to create a fake language with real linguistic principles.

Primary Books and Media: *Earthsong (Native Tongue III)* by Suzette Haden Elgin; *The Klingon Dictionary* by Mark Okrand; *The Art of Language Invention: From Horse-Lords to Dark Elves, the Words behind World-Building* by David J. Peterson; clips of Elvish from *The Lord of the Rings* movies; clips of Dothraki or other languages from *Game of Thrones* (TV series); clips of Klingon from *Star Trek: The Next Generation* or *Star Trek: Deep Space Nine* (TV series).

Additional Books and Media: There are Klingon Web resources available here: http://www.klingonwiki.net/En/AlienLanguagePrimer and http://deyvid-qonos.blogspot.com/2011/09/brief-introduction-to-klingon-language.html. You can also search for similar resources for many constructed and science-fiction languages. While Google Translate does not yet feature conlangs, Microsoft's search engine, Bing, does have a "translate into Klingon" feature. If using the Suzette Haden Elgin examples from her *Native Tongue* series, use this Web resource about Láadan: http://www.laadanlanguage.org/node/7.

Learning Objectives: Participants will

- Examine grammar rules of invented languages
- Understand the real linguistic constraints on invented languages
- Practice translating a few sentences into a fictional language

Duration: 2 hours

Materials Needed:

- Tablet/computer for watching clips and viewing language resources

Instructions:

- Show examples of Klingon, Elvish, or Dothraki language from the resources listed above. It is most helpful if you have written resources (say, a familiar saying or something like a children's rhyme in the target language) alongside video clips of actors and actresses speaking and performing the language from a TV series or movie, and also secondary (grammar, phonetics, vocabulary, etc.) resources from a print dictionary (like Okrand's Klingon dictionary or Web resources listed above).
- Ask participants to name any fictional languages they might be familiar with from TV shows or movies they like. Prompt them with examples from *Star Trek*, *Game of Thrones*, or Tolkien's books, if desired.
- Either pick a specific target conlang, or remain language agnostic and encourage participants to each chose a language to research and study.
- Walk students through the background of creating a fictional language, and show clips from *Trekkies* of Klingon language lessons. Ask them:
  - Why would fans spend so much time and energy creating an entirely artificial language?
  - How are these languages like real human languages, and how are they different?
  - How do these languages contribute to setting, characterization, and world building?
  - How does one (in the fictional world of the show or in real life) write these languages? Do they have their own alphabets? Do they have multiple alphabets to choose from, as do some real human languages such as Japanese?
- Guide participants to conlang.org and especially the map located by browsing to "conlangers map" or this link: https://www.google

.com/maps/d/u/0/edit?msa=0&ie=UTF&mid=18GpsMKaKmmT
_iQLB_mRdpwh4EO8.
  • Ask them to research their language and identify up to five re-
    sources for it.
• Direct group members to look up and learn 10 or so words in their
  new language, and also to learn one or two grammatical features
  that are different from English. Prompt them to consider how fictional cultures related to these languages affect the vocabulary and
  usage. For example, Klingon and Dothraki are both languages of
  warrior cultures. This means they often do not have direct translations
  of things like "please" or "thank you" or other forms of polite address.
  Sometimes, in conlangs, this ends up being silly and stereotypical, but
  it is also a marker of committed world building that seeks even to
  align the languages to the conflict and characterization.
• Participants can continue searching for resources, practicing their
  new conlangs, or teaching each other new words and phrases.
  Challenge them to find translations for the same set of concepts:
  library, circulation desk, search engines, board games, science
  fiction, and so forth.
• Consider using the map listed above to identify a real-life conlanger
  to invite as a guest to this program. He or she may be able to make a
  short presentation *in* or *about* the conlang. There are also many You-
  Tube videos of people speaking in or about artificial languages they,
  or others, have created.
• If desired, and with an expanded duration, challenge participants to
  create linguistic features of their own constructed languages. They
  can start with vocabulary, the sounds, the grammar, or the meanings.

Galactapedia Entry

Tame Wikipedia one-stop shoppers with this hilarious and entertaining program, where they practice writing in the formal style of an encyclopedia entry, make up a zany person, place, or thing, and begin a conversation about critical evaluation of sources and claims. Some teens might be inspired to begin editing or sourcing Wikipedia articles with library resources, which would be an excellent and useful enrichment activity.

Goals: To learn about Douglas Adams's seminal sci-fi classic, *The Hitchhiker's Guide to the Galaxy*, and reflect how (fictional) encyclopedias and travel guides can be used in fiction to create realistic setting and world building.

Primary Books and Media: *Missing Links and Secret Histories* by L. Timmel Duchamp; *The Hitchhiker's Guide to the Galaxy* by Douglas Adams.

Additional Books and Media: *Noggin* by John Corey Whaley; *Archivist Wasp* by Nicole Kornher-Stace.

Learning Objectives: Participants will

- Write and edit a Wikipedia-style encyclopedia entry
- Practice research and editing skills

Duration: 2 hours

Materials Needed:

- A sampling of travel guides
- Computer access or printouts of Wikipedia entries as samples

Instructions:

- Read the first few chapters of *The Hitchhiker's Guide to the Galaxy*, being sure to include examples where the text hews closely to the form of a travel guide.

- Make available photocopies of one of the stories in the Duchamp book, or versions of actual Wikipedia or fan wiki articles.
- This program is a study in form, and participants should become familiar with the form of the travel guide or Wikipedia entry by close reading examples from Adams and other sources.
- Challenge participants to think about the travel guides they have read. Distribute travel guides of real places to use as additional samples.
- Tell them that they are responsible for writing an article for the *Galactapedia*, a universal and massive shared knowledge compendium that reaches across the known intelligent species of the galaxy. Each participant should create a topic and write up to 500 words describing it. If they want, they can attempt to tell a story in the entry in the ways Adams and Duchamp's anthology do.
- Brainstorm possible topics:
  - Famous historical figures
  - Places: famous and beautiful cities, sites of battles, houses of historical interest, interesting geographical features, and so forth
  - Climate, science, and nature
  - Weird plants of the galaxy, both wild and domesticated
  - Animals, aliens, monsters, and so on
- Encourage them to be silly and wild. Their choice might be quite fantastical, but they should write an encyclopedia-type article about it as though it were real and serious.
- Spend up to an hour drafting and refining the drafts of students. Return constantly to the example entries, especially in terms of tone/diction and style, as well as in terms of what content to cover for a particular item.

Out of This World Book Club

Books clubs are library standards, for sure, but these clubs encourage wide participation and, if possible, should include a book to keep for every member. My greatest successes with book clubs in the library have been to read aloud large sections of the text at hand and then focus the discussion and activities on those sections. This promotes attendance from even reluctant or anxious readers, and makes it interactive. Sometimes, participants will want to take turns reading paragraphs or pages aloud, too. And, serve snacks!

Goals: To create a sustained teen or adult book club with contemporary, unusual, and/or exceptional and thought-provoking books that represent and speak to diverse audiences.

Primary Books and Media: (*Note:* See individual chapters on each book for discussion questions and extensions.) *The Girl in the Road* by Monica Byrne; *The Mount* by Carol Emshwiller; *The Summer Prince* by Alaya Dawn Johnson; *The Mirage* by Matt Ruff; *China Mountain Zhang* by Maureen McHugh; *All the Birds in the Sky* by Charlie Jane Anders; *Air* by Geoff Ryman; *The Best of All Possible Worlds* by Karen Lord; *The Devourers* by Indra Das; *Barsk: The Elephants' Graveyard* by Lawrence Schoen.

Additional Books and Media: Any; see examples below for ideas about developing discussion questions and extension activities for additional books.

Learning Objectives: Participants will

- Engage deeply with a longer, novel-length sci-fi or fantasy book
- Join a reading community

Duration: Several hours over several weeks, depending on group size. If possible, meeting for at least 1 hour twice a week is ideal, until you finish the book.

Materials Needed:

- Enough copies of the chosen book for each participant.
- If you wish to have participants do sketching, you may want to provide paper and pencils, or ask them to bring their own. Alternatively, sketches might be done in a computer program, in which case you'll need to have computer devices available.

The Girl in the Road
by Monica Byrne

This near-future novel features an unreliable narrator on the run from her life. As she is traveling on foot from India to Ethiopia (on an incredible offshore bridge structure that captures the energy of the ocean for human use), interpolated chapters tell an almost mythical story of a girl traveling the opposite direction. Byrne's world building and imagination of technology, especially nanotechnology, microbiology, and medicine, as well as advanced uses for solar energy, are dazzling.

Discussion Questions:

1. What is the chief job of a first-person narrator? Do you think you can trust this one?
2. The supposed division between Western medicine/science and Ayurvedic medicine is key to the medical science depicted in this book. What role does each play in the modern medicine of this world?
3. What of the futuristic technology in this book would you most like to have? What does this book say about the relationship between technology, people, and the natural world?

Extension Activities:

1. Make a map of the route.
2. Eat some of the food the narrator makes in her solar kitchen; find and print out pictures of any of the foods she eats or mentions.
3. Research Ayurvedic medicine in a library database or trusted Internet source. Try PubMed (http://www.ncbi.nlm.nih.gov/pubmed).

The Mount by Carol Emshwiller

This creepy future of humanity finds Earth much changed by a species of small, vicious aliens with extraordinarily strong hands and arms. They ride people like we do horses, and do all that comes with the treatment of farm animals, including breeding, training, punishing, and so forth. Emshwiller's startlingly clear prose and control of language makes readers forget they are reading about humans, and not horses, at all. By the end, the aliens are more sympathetic than you can imagine, and human readers are left pondering what it means to be an animal.

Discussion Questions:

1. Have you ridden horses? What was it like? Do you think it was really like the experience in this book?
2. Political revolution is a theme in this novel. Can you relate it to any contemporary events: civil wars, terrorist activities, civil disobedience, or other protest activities? What is the same in this world as in ours?
3. Emshwiller uses language in such a way that we are convinced we are reading about horses, not about people. What are some of the words and phrases that recur that help her achieve that?

Extension Activities:

1. Research the history of horse riding and the development of tools and technologies like bridles, stirrups, and so forth.
2. Draw the aliens.
3. Imagine you are a human in this world when the aliens arrive: write a diary entry from the point of view of someone who was there during first contact.

The Summer Prince by Alaya Dawn Johnson

Teens will be very comfortable reading this novel about creative and daring young people in a future Brazil where body modification is art, people are free to love people of all genders, reality TV and social media are melded into one strong social force, and the seeming utopia descends into terrifying dystopia with alarming regularity. The novel's title comes from a character who is chosen in a twisted version of *American Idol* or *America's Got Talent*, treated like a prince for a special season, and then sacrificed on live TV by the government. In addition, subplots about public art, romantic angst, and ecological change in humanity's near future make for a fascinating and heartbreaking world.

Discussion Questions:

1. This book is ostensibly about a culture based on matriarchy. What does Johnson achieve by having women in power, both in families and in this society?
2. How does the geography of the city and the ocean play into the conflict structure of the story? What is it about the setting that makes us believe these things are real?
3. In light of the way the novel starts with the televised ritual, what role does media and social media play in this story?

Extension Activities:

1. Research the history and practice of henna designs on skin, and practice them if you have the materials.
2. Research public art, especially Banksy and art pranks. Are there elements of the art protests in the book that are similar to something like Dismaland (http://www.thisiscolossal.com/2015/08/dismaland/)?
3. Research women heads of state. Which countries had the first women leaders? How many countries currently have women heads of state or heads of government?

The Mirage by Matt Ruff

This novel is a version of alternate history that centers around our current reality. In this alternate present, Christian religious fundamentalist terrorists from rural Colorado have flown two planes into the Twin Towers in a city in democratic Arabia, the world's superpower, a united states of Arab countries. In this timeline, there's a Jewish state in Germany, and what would be the United States is a politically divided set of developing-world societies. It gets much more complicated than that, and much weirder, too, as the reality of that alternate present begins collapsing into ours, organized around this desert metaphor of a mirage. This novel is provocative, especially about global politics, the American wars in the Middle East since 2003, and the intersections between Christianity and Islam.

Discussion Questions:

1. What are the key elements of history that are different in this book than in our real world? What is the most surprising difference?
2. What do you think Ruff is trying to achieve by "flipping" the world on its head in the way he does in this story?
3. What effect does it have on a reader to read about real-life characters, albeit their alternate history versions? Do you recognize these people from our world?

Extension Activities:

1. Draw a new world map that charts the setting and action of this novel.
2. Read *Osama* by Lavie Tidhar as an additional, comparative novel.
3. Write a news article about a current event from the perspective and setting of the world in this novel.

China Mountain Zhang by Maureen McHugh

McHugh's sensitive style and attunement to daily life and its struggles make this novel as emotionally prophetic as it is with the world economy, predicting China's ascendance to the point where the United States is a client state of China, and where Chinese Americans seek nothing more than a spot at a Chinese university or work posting so they can become successful participants in the economy. This world is a sophisticated look at what it would mean for the United States to no longer be a superpower, dramatized on the individual scale. The main character is also a gay man hiding and negotiating his sexual identity for these same economic and cultural reasons, who, importantly, remains an emotionally verifiable human rather than a symbol. There is a minor subplot about a Mars frontierswoman that foregrounds McHugh's feminist themes and realistically casts living on Mars a bit like living in the middle of the remote Arizona desert and demonstrates the breadth of McHugh's expansive and inspiring imagination.

Discussion Questions:

1. Zhang's gayness is sometimes at the forefront of the novel and sometimes not. If you were Zhang, would you be "out" about your sexuality? Why or why not? When and when not?
2. What do you think of a future United States that is a "cultural client" of China? Could you imagine this happening? Why or why not?
3. The kite racer is a motif and character that only recurs a few times in this book. What do you think McHugh's intention was with that character and situation?

Extension Activities:

1. Research Chinese territorial expansion over the last 100 years, and draw a map.

2. Draw a picture of the settlement on Mars.
3. Write a diary entry as though you were in a neighboring settlement in rural Mars. What would your life be like?

All the Birds in the Sky
by Charlie Jane Anders

Anders spent many years as the editor of the popular sci-fi and media blog io9.com, and this, her debut novel, both gazes inward at fandom and always charts a bold new path. The story effortlessly blends traditional elements of science fiction and fantasy in a manner that both explicitly dramatizes a conflict between nature and magic on the one hand and science and technology on the other and self-consciously plays with tropes and patterns of both traditions to tell a convincing story about witches, artificial intelligence, and a San Francisco being gentrified by tech bros. One of the few novels that realistically follows teenagers as they turn into adults, this book draws its readers into a world of misfits, outcasts, and weirdos, and makes them all the more glad for it.

Discussion Questions:

1. Is Patricia's power accidental? In what ways is she like a prototypical fantasy hero "chosen one" who naively engages at the beginning, but triumphs in the end?
2. What do you think Anders is saying about the relationship between science and magic? Is it the same thing she is trying to communicate about intersections and overlaps between science fiction and fantasy?
3. If you were a character in this novel, would you be one of the witches or one of the technologists? Why?

Extension Activities:

1. Write spells that Patricia and her colleagues might have used.
2. Make a Google map of the San Francisco and Bay Area locations featured in this book.
3. Cast this book! Imagine that you are the casting director for the adaption of this book into a movie or miniseries. Who would you recommend play the lead roles, and why?

Air by Geoff Ryman

In *Air*, the world is about to all go online, all at once, inside people's heads
—digital connectivity appearing everywhere, in everyone's brains.
A failed test of this new system (Air) leaves the main character's village
disoriented and motivated to modernize and find ways to connect to the
wider world. This novel dramatizes globalization in a science-fiction
way by concentrating on Chung Mae's world and how she leverages digital literacy, entrepreneurship, creativity, and boldness to better herself
and her community. There are numerous entry points to this story, including the digital literacy gap in poor and rural America, the fictional central
Asian country depicted in this book, and how women find power and ful-
fillment even within rigid traditions and rules structured to limit them.

Discussion Questions:

1. When did you all first go online? Forty-year-olds probably did it first
   when they were young teenagers, but what about kids today? Are your
   grandparents online? What is the Internet and navigating social media
   like for them?
2. What are some of the things Mae does online that you also do online?
3. How is life different in the village depicted in this novel from the way
   you live? Are your houses different? Food? Transportation? Economy?
   Make a compare/contrast list.

Extension Activities:

1. Research digital inclusion in Central and Southeast Asia. What are the
   rates of broadband adoption compared to the United States, Canada,
   or Europe?
2. Draw a portrait of Mae.
3. Research current developments in wearable technology, virtual reality,
   and augmented reality (like Google Glass). Are these things putting us
   on the path to "Air"?

The Best of All Possible Worlds
by Karen Lord

Lord's novel seems inspired by SF master Ursula K. Le Guin, who leveraged her expertise in anthropology, sociology, and language to create some of the most alien humans in the genre. Many of Le Guin's books are part of the Hainish cycle, in which humans have seeded hundreds or thousands of worlds in the galaxy over thousands of years. While there has been some genetic divergence, there has been even more cultural reinvention, where everything from marital customs and gender identity to food customs varies. Lord's book dramatizes a similar concept all on one world; in the aftermath of an annihilating galactic war, several species of humans find themselves coexisting on one planet. From strong telepaths and violent telekinetics to a community obeying the rules of the Faery from our contemporary fantasy tradition of fairies and faery, Delarua, the main character, experiences many different varieties of people. On top of this richly built world is a futurist governmental and scientific procedural as Delarua and her crew travel around the planet on a survey team. The diverse team is a microcosm of the societies in this novel, and provides sometimes tedious dramatization of the differences between these species of humans. Delarua eventually experiences romance, but only after a family trauma that underscores the consequences at play in this world.

Discussion Questions:

1. Are the different human cultures in this novel believable? Which are more believable? Are there any cultures you are familiar with who are so uniform? Why do you think the author created these cultural differences? What did she want to express?
2. Psychic powers are very dangerous in this novel. What do you make of the sad story of Delarua's sister's family? How did you feel about Ioan? What do you think the author wanted you to feel?

3. This novel contemplates how a culture might move on from war and
    genocide. What are their strategies? Do you think they are working?
    What do you think might work better?

Extension Activities:

1. Read Hainish cycle stories or novels, especially "Mountain Ways,"
    reprinted at *Clarkesworld* (http://clarkesworldmagazine.com/le_guin_
    03_14_reprint/) or in *The Birthday of the World*. What are some of the
    similarities or differences between the diverse human cultures in that
    story and in this one?
2. Draw a world map of where this novel takes place. Show which parts
    of the novel take place in which territories.
3. Draw a character wheel for this story, with a portrait/image of each
    main character and lines showing how they are related to each other
    (friend, colleague, lover, spouse, enemy, etc.).

The Devourers by Indra Das

This debut novel is a fabulist palimpsest of stories that nestle on stories made real by several mysterious and symbolic manuscripts, some of which are even written on the skins of primary characters. _The Devourers_ is a story of queer desire as much as ancient stories about werewolves and their many incarnations throughout Europe and Asia. Language takes the forefront in this book, and there are several extended passages that operate only on a metaphysical and metaphorical level and that cannot exist literally. These flights of style demand a lot of the reader, but Das delivers with an emotionally relevant and contemporary gay love story in our present while convincingly describing centuries of violence and desire.

Discussion Questions:

1. Desire plays a fundamental role in why these various characters come together or not. What do you make of the different kinds of desire (physical, hunger/thirst, sexual, revenge) displayed by these characters?
2. The stories in this novel are layered upon each other like a palimpsest, each story a leaf that can be peeled back to reveal another story. Why did the author chose this structure? Why is so much of this story in the form of texts written by characters?
3. This novel also plays with the idea of reliability/unreliability of the narrator, grounded in the central question that it begins with: Is this a real werewolf or just some person who believes he is a werewolf or wants others to believe that? What do you make of this unreliability? Were you convinced they were actual werewolves? When and why?

Extension Activities:

1. Research the various werewolf traditions explicitly referenced in this novel: loup-garou, shapeshifters, and so forth.

2. Read *Liar* by Justine Larbalestier and compare and contrast the narrative techniques of the novels, especially in terms of reliability and unreliability of the narrator.
3. Research the history of precolonial India and the Mughal Empire, especially its trade—cultural and economic—with other parts of Asia and Europe.

Barsk: The Elephants' Graveyard by Lawrence Schoen

This extraordinary novel starts with funeral customs of beings who are sentient elephants—that is, beings with the heads of elephants and humanoid bodies—who exist in a universe where other animals with human bodies travel on spaceships and form an intergalactic civilization. It turns out the elephants are one of the backward elevated animal races, existing in a kind of preserve while the creatures who are bears, leopards, and other animals govern. This is a fascinating far-future extrapolation of what genetic engineering could wreak, and tells very human stories about death and loss in the guise of a completely alien, elephant culture.

Discussion Questions:

1. Which "elevated animal" culture would you most like to belong to, and why?
2. This book is a mixture of pre-technological fantasy and science fiction. What are the elements of each mode of this novel, that is, what are the setting and detail ingredients that Schoen uses to indicate the differences between these two layers of this novel?
3. If you were able to have a conversation with someone or some being long dead and from a very different time than yours, who would it be and why?

Extension Activities:

1. Research death and funeral cultures from around the world. Are there any human rituals that resemble what the Fant of Barsk do?
2. Draw a couple panels of a graphic novel adaptation of this book.
3. What additional animals would you "elevate" if you were in charge of this world? Why would you add them?

Appendix A

Science Fiction and Fantasy for the Very Young (Preschool Programming)

USING SCIENCE FICTION

Science fiction picture books offer you a great way to expose preschoolers to science concepts and add an extra dimension to these story times, and it is a space for imaginations to run wild. There is so much of the fantastical in picture books that I like to use real science as core themes for preschoolers. The following program plans stretch out science-SFF hybrid programs that use both to maximum effect with the very young.

You can gauge your audience, of course, but it's also important to say something like, "This is a pretend story about traveling to the moon. The last story was about looking at the moon carefully from Earth. A few people have been to the moon, and they are called astronauts."

OBSERVING THE MOON

Books

Moonlight by Helen Griffith
Faces of the Moon by Bob Crelin
A Full Moon Is Rising: Poems by Marilyn Singer

Songs/Fingerplays

We're Flying to the Moon

We're flying to the moon
Oh, what an adventure,
We're flying to the moon!

Ten, nine, eight, seven, six, five,
Four, three, two, and one: Blast off!!

I watch the stars come out at night (look up)

I wonder where they get their light (shrug shoulders)
I don't think they'll ever fall (shake head "no")
So I'll reach up and pick them all! (pretend to pick stars from the sky)

Activities

Oreo Phases of the Moon: Separate sandwich cookies and use a plastic knife or craft stick to scrape away the frosting until you have samples of a new moon, a quarter moon, a half moon, a three-quarters moon, and a full moon. (See http://observethemoonnight.org/activities/.)

Rotation in Action: You be the sun, pick one child to be the moon, and everyone else is the Earth. As the moon follows a complete circle around you (as the sun), ask everyone to imagine what part(s) of the moon they can see. Remind them that the "slice" they can see from their one spot on Earth matches up to the shapes of the moon they recognize.

BALANCE

Books

Balancing Act by Ellen Stoll Walsh
Little Yoga: A Toddler's First Book of Yoga by Rebecca Whitford
Flora and the Flamingo by Molly Idle

Songs/Fingerplays

Smooth Road

Smooth road, smooth road, smooth road
Bumpy road, bumpy road, bumpy road
Rough road, rough road, rough road,
Hole!

Tall as a Tree

As tall as a tree. (Arms up, toes digging in like roots)
As wide as a house. (Arms stretched wide, deep voice)
Skinny as a pole. (Stand to side, squeaky, thin voice)
As small as a mouse. (Curl up into a ball and make mouse noise.)

Finger on Your Nose

Put one finger on your nose,
And another on your toes.
Now put the finger on your nose on your toes,
And the finger on your toes on your nose.
Without moving your fingers, try to sit down!

Activities

Center of Gravity: Put a pencil about three feet in front of participants, and challenge them to pick it up without moving their feet. Even yogis will either fall or move their feet because their center of balance moves too far away from their feet. Explain that balance means keeping your center of gravity supported and stable.

Pencil Trick: Balance an unsharpened pencil across the back of one or two fingers. Find the place where the pencil's center of gravity is stable!

Imaginary Seesaw: Inspired by Walsh's *Balancing Act*, act out an imaginary seesaw by splitting children into two groups and adding or subtracting them one by one. Make sure the "heavier" side bends down and the "lighter" side reaches up their arms as you add children.

PLANT SCIENCE

Books

Up, Down, and Around by Katherine Ayres
The Carrot Seed by Ruth Krauss
The Tiny Seed by Eric Carle

Songs/Fingerplays

This is the way we plant the seeds,
Plant the seeds, plant the seeds,
This is the way we plant the seeds,
Early in the springtime.

This is the way we dig the hole ...
This is the way we put in the seeds ...
This is the way we cover the seeds ...
This is the way we water the seeds ...
This is the way we check the seeds ...

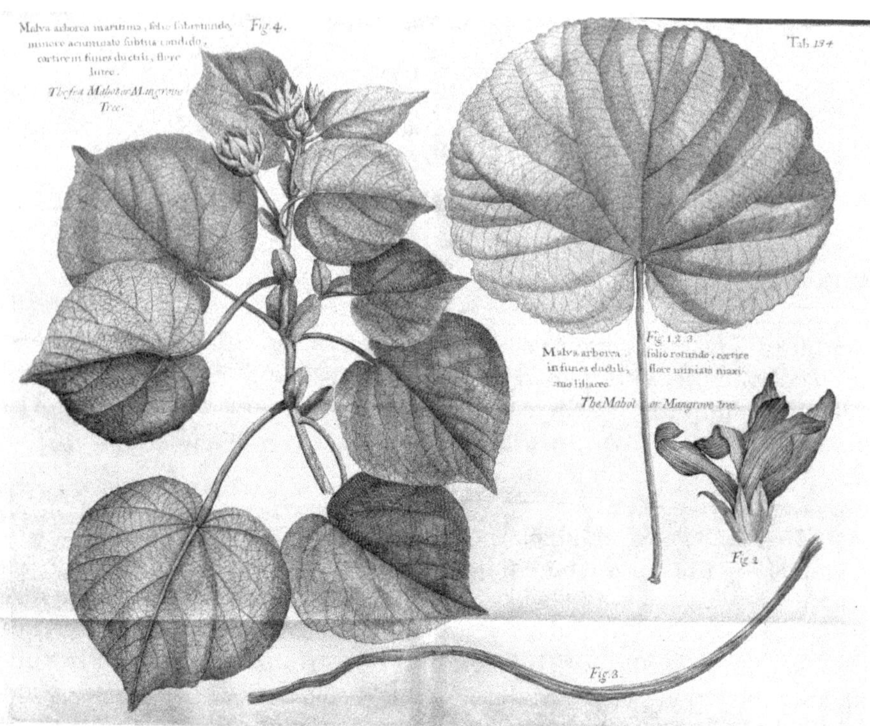

Courtesy of Biodiversity Heritage Library. https://www.flickr.com/photos/
biodivlibrary/21300957536/in/album-72157658485136281/.

Five fat peas in a pea pod pressed

One grew, two grew, so did all the rest
They grew and grew and did not stop until one pea in the pod went POP!

Activities

Seeds of All Sizes: From sesame to avocado, bring in as many seeds as
you can find and let participants touch them. What different textures do
they feel? How big are these different seeds?

Seed Starts: Start any quick-growing seeds, like mung beans, in recycled
containers to send home or keep on the windowsill in the library.

Appendix B

Outcomes Evaluation

All library programs should include an evaluation component that helps the practitioners gauge whether or not they are effectively meeting the needs of their users and participants and also to help measure the impact of these programs. Traditionally, libraries have counted the number of programs and the attendance. I encourage you to measure those indicators, but also to think about demonstrating whether or not your programming has changed someone's attitudes or might have some impact on a participant's behavior.

One additional measure to frame this assessment could be recurring attendance, that is, how many participants come back time after time, if you decide to run several of these program plans in a science fiction and fantasy series. Use and save sign-in sheets if you decide to track this.

The evaluation that can determine the impact of your programming is outcomes evaluation. See the excellent and compact *Five Steps of Outcome-Based Planning and Evaluation for Public Libraries* by Melissa Gross, Cindy Mediavilla, and Virginia A. Walter for a more complete explanation of the process of outcomes evaluation.

Additionally, the Public Library Association's initiative Project Outcome (https://www.projectoutcome.org/) can help libraries of all sizes start assessing their impact by demonstrating outcomes in users. Below are two sample outcomes surveys. They should be administered before and after each program. Over time, the many pre-surveys or pre-tests and their corresponding post-tests may demonstrate that your program is having a positive impact. As is stressed in the Gross et al. title referenced above, it is crucial to identify outcomes based on community need and what you determine the program has a chance of impacting. In the sample surveys below, the outcomes are about reading: increasing volume of reading, increasing enjoyment of reading, and increasing reading confidence. There is also a question about finding things to read that speaks more directly to any outcomes around the child's information-seeking behaviors in the library.

SAMPLE SURVEY FOR CHILDREN

How often do you read by yourself?

a. Every day   b. Once or twice a week   c. Less than once a week

How often do you read with someone else (parent, brother, sister, other family member)?

a. Every day   b. Once or twice a week   c. Less than once a week

I like reading

1   2   3   4   5   6   7   8   9   10
Not at all   Somewhat   A lot

I feel like I am good at reading

1   2   3   4   5   6   7   8   9   10
Not at all   Somewhat   A lot

I know how to find things I like to read

1   2   3   4   5   6   7   8   9   10
Not at all   Somewhat   A lot

SAMPLE SURVEY FOR PARENTS

How often does your child read to himself or herself?

a. Every day   b. Once or twice a week   c. Less than once a week

How much does your child enjoy reading?

1   2   3   4   5   6   7   8   9   10
Not at all   Somewhat   A lot

How did your child do on his or her last report card?

1   2   3   4   5   6   7   8   9   10

He/she struggled   He/she did just OK   He/she did great   He/she excelled

Would you be willing to participate in a quick phone call to follow up in a few months?

Yes   No

Name: ____

Please tell us a good number we can use to reach you: ________________

Bibliography

Adams, Douglas. *The Hitchhiker's Guide to the Galaxy*. New York: Harmony, 1980.

Anders, Charlie Jane. *All the Birds in the Sky*. New York: Tor Books, 2016.

Anderson, M. T. *Feed*. Cambridge, MA: Candlewick, 2002.

Asimov, Isaac. *I, Robot*. New York: Bantam, 2004.

Atwood, Margaret. *Good Bones and Simple Murders*. New York: Nan A. Talese, Doubleday, 1994.

Atwood, Margaret. *The Handmaid's Tale*. Boston: Houghton Mifflin, 1986.

Atwood, Margaret. *Oryx and Crake: A Novel*. New York: Anchor, 2004.

Ayres, Katherine, and Nadine Bernard Westcott. *Up, Down, and Around*. Cambridge, MA: Candlewick, 2007.

Barnes, Steven. *Zulu Heart*. New York: Warner, 2003.

Bear, Greg. *Nebula Awards Showcase 2015: Stories, Excerpts, and Poems: The Year's Best Science Fiction and Fantasy*. Amherst, NY: PYR, an Imprint of Prometheus Books, 2015.

Bennett, Robert Jackson. *City of Stairs: A Novel*. New York: Broadway Books, 2014.

Black, Holly. *The Coldest Girl in Coldtown*. New York: Little, Brown Books for Young Readers, 2013.

Black, Holly. *White Cat*. New York: Margaret K. McElderry, 2010.

Bradbury, Ray. *Dinosaur Tales*. Toronto: Bantam, 1983.

Brennan, Marie. *A Natural History of Dragons: A Memoir by Lady Trent*. New York: Tor, 2013.

Bujold, Lois McMaster. *Cordelia's Honor*. Riverdale, NY: Baen, 1999.

Butler, Octavia E. *Bloodchild and Other Stories*. New York: Four Walls Eight Windows, 1995.

Butler, Octavia E. *Fledgling*. New York: Seven Stories, 2005.

Butler, Octavia E., and Enric Torres-Prat. *Dawn: Xenogenesis*. New York: Warner, 1987.

Byrne, Monica. *The Girl in the Road*. New York: Crown Publishers, 2014.

Cambias, James L. *A Darkling Sea.* New York: Tor, 2014.

Carle, Eric. *The Tiny Seed.* Natick, MA: Picture Book Studio, 1987.

Carter, Angela. *The Bloody Chamber, and Other Stories.* New York: Penguin, 1993.

Collins, Suzanne. *The Hunger Games.* New York: Scholastic Press, 2008.

Corey, James S. A. *Leviathan Wakes.* New York: Orbit, 2011.

Cormier, Robert. *I Am the Cheese.* New York: Knopf, 1977.

Crelin, Bob, and Leslie Evans. *Faces of the Moon.* Watertown, MA: Charlesbridge, 2009.

Crichton, Michael. *Jurassic Park: A Novel.* New York: Knopf, 1990.

Cronin, Justin. *The Passage: A Novel.* New York: Ballantine, 2010.

Das, Indra. *The Devourers.* New York: Del Rey, 2016.

Delany, Samuel R. *About Writing: Seven Essays, Four Letters, and Five Interviews.* Middletown, CT: Wesleyan UP, 2005.

Doctorow, Cory. *Little Brother.* New York: Tor Books, 2008.

Doctorow, Cory. *Pirate Cinema.* New York: Tor Books, 2012.

Doctorow, Cory, Amanda Palmer, and Neil Gaiman. *Information Doesn't Want to Be Free: Laws for the Internet Age.* San Francisco: McSweeney's, 2015.

Dorsey, Candas Jane. *A Paradigm of Earth.* New York: Tor, 2001.

Duchamp, L. Timmel, ed. *Missing Links and Secret Histories: A Selection of Wikipedia Entries from Across the Known Multiverse.* Seattle: Aqueduct, 2013.

Dyckman, Ame, and Dan Yaccarino. *Boy + Bot.* New York: Alfred A. Knopf, 2012.

Elgin, Suzette Haden. *Earthsong.* New York: Feminist, 2002.

Ellison, Harlan, and Isaac Asimov. *I, Robot: The Illustrated Screenplay.* New York: Warner, 1994.

Emshwiller, Carol. *The Mount: A Novel.* Brooklyn: Small Beer, 2002.

Geisert, Arthur. *The Giant Seed.* New York: Enchanted Lion, 2012.

Geisert, Arthur. *Ice.* Brooklyn: Enchanted Lion, 2011.

Grahame-Smith, Seth. *Abraham Lincoln: Vampire Hunter.* New York: Grand Central Pub., 2010.

Green, John, and David Levithan. *Will Grayson, Will Grayson.* New York: Dutton, 2010.

Griffith, Helen V., and Laura Dronzek. *Moonlight.* New York: Greenwillow, 2012.

Griffith, Nicola. *Hild.* New York: Farrar, Straus and Giroux, 2013.

Grossman, Lev. *The Magicians: A Novel.* New York: Viking, 2009.

Huff, Tanya, John Barrowman, Sigrid Ellis, Michael Damian Thomas, and Paul Magrs. *Queers Dig Time Lords: A Celebration of Doctor Who by the LGBTQ Fans Who Love It.* Des Moines: Mad Norwegian, 2013.

Hughes, Emily. *The Little Gardener.* London: Flying Eye Books, 2015.

Idle, Molly Schaar. *Flora and the Flamingo.* San Francisco: Chronicle, 2013.

Ishiguro, Kazuo. *Never Let Me Go.* New York: Alfred A. Knopf, 2005.

Jackson, Shelley. *Half Life: A Novel.* New York: HarperCollins, 2006.

Jeffers, Oliver. *The Way Back Home.* New York: Philomel, 2008.

Jemisin, N. K. *The Fifth Season.* New York: Orbit, 2015.

Jemisin, N. K. The Inheritance Trilogy. Includes: *The Hundred Thousand Kingdoms, The Broken Kingdoms, The Kingdom of Gods,* and *The Awakened Kingdom.* New York: Orbit, 2014.

Johnson, Alaya Dawn. *The Summer Prince.* New York: Arthur A. Levine, 2013.

Krasnostein, Alisa, and Julia Rios. *Kaleidoscope: Diverse YA Science Fiction and Fantasy Stories.* Yokine, WA: Twelfth Planet Press, 2014.

Krauss, Ruth, and Crockett Johnson. *The Carrot Seed.* New York: Harper & Brothers, 1945.

Kushner, Ellen. *Swordspoint: A Novel.* New York: Arbor House, 1987.

Lackey, Mercedes. *Nebula Awards Showcase 2016: The Year's Best Science Fiction and Fantasy.* Amherst, NY: Pyr, 2016.

Lanagan, Margo. *Black Juice.* New York: Eos, 2005.

Lanagan, Margo. *Yellowcake.* New York: Knopf, 2013.

Larbalestier, Justine. *Liar.* New York: Bloomsbury U.S.A. Children's, 2009.

Leckie, Ann. *Ancillary Justice.* New York: Orbit, 2013.

Le Guin, Ursula K. *The Birthday of the World and Other Stories.* New York: HarperCollins, 2002.

Le Guin, Ursula K. *The Left Hand of Darkness.* New York: Ace, 2000.

Le Guin, Ursula K., and Ruth Robbins. *A Wizard of Earthsea.* Berkeley: Parnassus, 1968.

Lo, Malinda. *Ash.* New York: Little, Brown, 2009.

Lord, Karen. *The Best of All Possible Worlds: A Novel.* New York: Del Rey, Ballantine Books, 2013.

Martin, George R. R. *A Game of Thrones.* New York: Bantam Dell, 1996.

Martin, George R. R., and Gary Gianni, illustrator. *A Knight of the Seven Kingdoms.* New York: Bantam Books, 2015.

McHugh, Maureen F. *China Mountain Zhang.* New York: Tom Doherty Associates, 1992.

Miéville, China. *Perdido Street Station.* New York: Del Rey, 2001.

Miéville, China. *Three Moments of an Explosion: Stories.* New York: Del Rey, 2015.

Miller, Ron. *The Dream Machines: An Illustrated History of the Spaceship in Art, Science, and Literature.* Malabar, FL: Krieger Pub., 1993.

Montalvo-Lagos, Tomás, Michael Dante DiMartino, and Bryan Konietzko. *Avatar: The Last Airbender.* Hamburg: Tokyopop, 2006.

Moore, Alan, and Dave Gibbons. *Watchmen.* New York: DC Comics, 1987.

Morales, Yuyi. *Little Night.* New Milford, CT: Roaring Brook, 2007.

Myers, Walter Dean. *Monster.* New York: Harper Collins, 1999.

Niles, Steve, Ben Templesmith, and Robbie Robbins. *30 Days of Night.* San Diego: Idea & Design Works, LLC, 2003.

Okorafor, Nnedi. *Binti.* New York: Tom Doherty Associates, LLC, 2015.

Paolini, Christopher. *Eldest.* New York: Alfred A. Knopf, 2005.

Peterson, David J. *The Art of Language Invention: From Horse-Lords to Dark Elves, the Words behind World-building.* New York: Penguin Books, 2015.

Phillips, Julie. *James Tiptree, Jr.: The Double Life of Alice B. Sheldon.* New York: St. Martin's, 2006.

Priest, Cherie. *Dreadnought*. New York: Tor, 2010.

Pullman, Philip. *The Golden Compass*. New York: Knopf Books for Young Readers, 1996.

Resnick, Michael D. *A Miracle of Rare Design: A Tragedy of Transcendence*. New York: Tor, 1994.

Rice, Anne. *Interview with the Vampire*. New York: Knopf, 1976.

Ringgold, Faith. *Tar Beach*. New York: Crown, 1991.

Riordan, Rick. *The Kane Chronicles: The Complete Series*. New York: Disney/Hyperion, 2013.

Riordan, Rick. *The Red Pyramid*. New York: Disney/Hyperion, 2010.

Robertson, Scott, Daniel Gardner, and Annis Naeem. *Blast: Spaceship Sketches and Renderings*. London: Titan, 2012.

Rowling, J. K., and Mary GrandPré, illustrator. *Harry Potter: The Complete Series*. New York: Scholastic, 2009.

Ruff, Matt. *The Mirage*. New York: Harper, 2012.

Russ, Joanna. *The Female Man*. Boston: Beacon, 1986.

Russ, Joanna. *How to Suppress Women's Writing*. Austin: University of Texas, 1983.

Ryman, Geoff. *Air: Or, Have Not Have*. New York: St. Martin's Griffin, 2004.

Saunders, George. *Pastoralia: Stories*. New York: Riverhead, 2000.

Schoen, Lawrence M. *Barsk: The Elephants' Graveyard*. New York: Tor, 2015.

Selznick, Brian. *The Invention of Hugo Cabret: A Novel in Words and Pictures*. New York: Scholastic, 2007.

Shawl, Nisi. *Everfair*. New York: Tor, 2016.

Shawl, Nisi. *Filter House: Short Fiction*. Seattle: Aqueduct, 2008.

Shepard, Sara. *Pretty Little Liars*. New York: Harper Teen, 2007.

Singer, Marilyn, and Julia Cairns. *A Full Moon Is Rising: Poems*. New York: Lee & Low, 2011.

Swanwick, Michael. *The Dog Said Bow-Wow*. San Francisco: Tachyon Pub., 2007.

Thomas, Lynne M., and Tara O'Shea. *Chicks Dig Time Lords: A Celebration of Doctor Who by the Women Who Love It*. Des Moines: Mad Norwegian, 2010.

Thomson, Bill. *Chalk*. New York: Marshall Cavendish Children, 2010.

Tidhar, Lavie. *Osama: A Novel*. Oxford, U.K.: Solaris, 2012.

Tokyo SF Makeup Workshop. *A Complete Guide to Special Effects Makeup*. London: Titan, 2012.

VanderMeer, Ann, and Jeff VanderMeer. *Steampunk*. San Francisco: Tachyon Books, 2008.

Walton, Jo. *Among Others*. New York: Tor Books, 2011.

Walton, Jo. *What Makes This Book So Great*. New York: Tor Books, 2014.

Westerfeld, Scott. *Afterworlds*. New York: Simon and Schuster, 2014.

Westerfeld, Scott. *Leviathan*. New York: Simon and Schuster, 2009.

Wilson, Kai Ashante. *The Sorcerer of the Wildeeps*. Tor.com, 2015. Kindle edition.

Wolfe, Brian and Nick. *Extreme Costume Makeup: 25 Creepy & Cool Step-by-Step Demos*. Cincinnati: Impact Books, 2013.

Woodson, Jacqueline. *Brown Girl Dreaming*. New York: Penguin Books, 2014.

Index

About the Author

Joel A. Nichols is the author of *iPads® in the Library: Using Tablet Technology to Enhance Programs for All Ages* (Libraries Unlimited, 2013) and *Teaching Internet Basics: The Can-Do Guide* (Libraries Unlimited, 2014). He is the data strategy and evaluation administrator at the Free Library of Philadelphia, and regularly speaks and writes about technology programming, queer and genderqueer library services, and library strategy and assessment. He was previously children's librarian and branch manager at a neighborhood library in Philadelphia, and also managed the Free Library Techmobile, a digital literacy outreach vehicle. He has an MSLIS from Drexel University, an MA in creative writing and English from Temple University, and a BA in German from Wesleyan University. He grew up in Vermont, and lives in Philadelphia with his partner and their child.